Praise fo

"A visionary storyteller'

In Cheshire Magazine.

Praise for Inside The Cheshire Set

"The funniest, wittiest novel this decade."

Manchester Evening News

"Sex, drugs and depravity."

Cheshire Life

"Well written, fast paced and has some real laugh out loud moments... a fascinating peek behind the gaudy veneer of life in Cheshire.

Amazon.co.uk

Praise for The Tenants

"Full of home truths and told in such a memorable tale. Thoroughly enjoyed this book"

Amazon.co.uk

"An honest, simple mirror of liberation that we all need in our 'want it, have it, want it' lives."

Amazon.co.uk

BLACK

A NOVEL

MALCOLM STORER

EMPIRE
PUBLICATIONS

EMPIRE PUBLICATIONS
1 Newton St., Manchester M1 1HW

ISBN: 9781915616234

I vow to thee my country

Sir Cecil Spring Rice

For Elisabetta

PART I

Before the Civil War

I

King William nervously paced the Audience Room of Buckingham Palace; the same room where, every Tuesday for seven decades, his grandmother had expertly guided over a dozen prime ministers. How the country needed her now.

It was his first audience with the new prime minister — with any prime minister — and he was woefully unprepared.

Weighed down by the affairs of state he walked past the window, stopping for a moment to gaze across the back lawn; the trees were starting to bud, a sight that had always cheered his nature-loving father. It had been two months since his assassination at the hands of an illegal migrant; two whirlwind months that had thrown the country into disarray and culminated in the election of a hard-line right-wing government. Bourne on a wave of fear, patriotism and sheer frustration at their political masters, the British people had turned their backs on the mainstream parties and elected the little-known GB Patriots, their charismatic leader Michael Taylor appearing Moses-like out of the political wilderness promising stability and a new beginning.

Following the general election, the Establishment — mindful of how close the country had come to anarchy and keen to instil a sense of unity in the population — was quick to promote this 'new beginning'. The majority of the media were also onboard, drawing parallels between the new monarch and the new prime minister — their youth and inexperience, their wholehearted patriotism — ensuring the nation's sympathy. Big business followed suit, relieved that the pound had finally rallied after falling to an all-time low following the death of King Charles.

The liberal-left media, however, realising they were skating on thin ice, were strangely silent, unsure of how best to deal with the descendent of a slave, a man the *Guardian* had once featured in an article entitled 'Britain's Top Black Lawyers', in which they trumpeted the UK's multi-racial society while at the same time insisting more should be done to further the cause of black people. To them Michael Taylor represented a kind of Frankenstein's monster that had somehow emerged out of the cultural landscape they themselves had created, and was hell-bent on destroying it. Not that the public took much notice; after years of supporting an open-door policy on immigration and cancelling anyone with differing views, the left were seen as complicit in the regicide, their political correctness consigned to the dustbin. A strange thing had happened to the British people since the assassination; a kind of political metamorphosis. After decades of government incompetence and corruption — the Iraq War, the Post Office and Infected Blood scandals — their centuries-long moderation suddenly snapped. We've had enough, was the message.

"Penny for your thoughts."

William had forgotten Katherine was in the room. He turned and saw her perched on the edge of the sofa, her face deathly pale and rigid with stress, her hands clutching her Smartphone. She noticed how worried he looked; he'd yet to be crowned king and already he was facing the biggest constitutional crises since the Second World War.

The young king faked a smile. "I was just thinking how nice the garden looks."

Katherine shot up and walked towards him, showing him her phone. "He's on his way."

William stared at the live newsfeed; a black Range Rover flanked by police outriders was heading up the Mall towards the Palace. Huge flag-bearing crowds lined the route, some waving Union Jacks, others the emblem of GB Patriots — a golden acorn on a sky-blue background.

"He's certainly popular."

"Especially with the ladies," said Katherine. "The British Obama they're calling him."

"From what I've seen on TV he certainly has his charm."

"What do the security services say about him?"

"There's no dirt, if that's what you mean. Divorced, a former defence barrister, he's squeaky clean. Not so much as a parking ticket… Look at that!"

The live-feed suddenly focused in on the crowd lining the Mall; instead of the usual sea of white faces, the crowd was an equal mix of black, white, South Asian and Chinese, all waving flags. "Seems to be pulling the country together. I've not seen such a diverse crowd since Harry and M…"

"Since Harry and Megan's wedding you mean... It's alright William, you can say her name." Katherine sighed, "Hard to believe it was only ten years ago… She's all over social media since he won the election you know, saying what a breath of fresh air he'll be for the country. Harry's followed suit of course, implying that Megan had somehow 'paved the way'."

William raised his eyes. "Quelle surprise."

A polite tap on the door. "Come in."

The king's private secretary entered the room, "Prime Minister Taylor will be here in three minutes your Majesty."

"Thank you, Martin."

Katherine kissed William on the cheek. "I'll go and see to the children." She gave his arm a gentle squeeze. "Good luck."

William watched his wife leave the room, her skinny frame testament to the enormous stress they'd both been under since his father's assassination, the details of which filled him with a profound sense of sadness.

During a visit to a migrant centre in Kent, King Charles was chatting to a group of new arrivals when twenty-three-year-old Abbas Abdulla from Mosel lunged at him with a kitchen knife, stabbing him repeatedly in the chest while screaming, "This is for Palestine!" The king was immediately rushed to hospital but died en-route. William was on a state visit to Cardiff at the time and was informed after addressing the Senedd.

William stood by the fireplace. He glanced at the walnut side table where a collection of today's newspapers were neatly laid out. THE PEOPLE'S CHOICE! was the headline in the *Daily Mail*. DESTINY CALLS, blared the *Telegraph*. Both newspapers had large, close-up photographs of Michael Taylor, his handsome face wreathed in a smile. The Sun ran with I HAVE A DREAM. Only the Guardian stood out, with its less than enthusiastic and circumspect THE COUNTRY EXPECTS.

Another polite knock at the door.

"Come in."

The king's private secretary entered the room. "Prime Minister Taylor, your Majesty."

"Send him in."

II

DUSK WAS FALLING as Michael parked his silver BMW in the Levenshulme branch of Sainsbury's. It meant walking half a mile or so but at least his pride and joy would be safe. He released the seatbelt and sat for a moment listening to his favourite song: 'Holding Back the Years' by Simple Red. Hucknall's voice captivated him; its emotional gravitas. When he first heard it on the radio all those years ago he was convinced the singer was black. He couldn't believe his eyes when he watched *Top of The Pops* and discovered the voice belonged to a ginger-haired white guy. Looks don't always reveal the truth about a person, his mother used to say.

He'd heard the song a million times, usually at his house in the Cotswolds or in his London flat or whatever glamorous part of the world he happen to be in. But now, back in Levenshulme after almost two decades, a stone's throw from where Mick Hucknall was born, the lyrics opened up a wound. Why that was, he couldn't say; he was a successful barrister married to a beautiful woman with two adorable children, so none of his thirty-eight years had been wasted as far as he could tell. Nevertheless, deep inside there was a void he'd never managed to fill.

As the song ebbed away a lump formed in his throat. *Get a grip!* He shoved his laptop under the passenger seat and glanced into the back for valuables. After checking himself in the rear-view mirror, he opened the driver's door. A young Asian couple parked next to him were loading their battered Clio with shopping. Urdu chatter. Michael cursed inwardly, *Speak English!* The Urdu ceased as if by magic and the couple stared at him, surprised to see a well-dressed black man — dark-blue pinstriped suit, black three-quarter length cashmere overcoat, polished black brogues, gold Rolex — stepping out of an expensive car. Michael returned their stares with a flash of disdain. *Got a problem?* The young couple looked away timidly. He turned his collar up against the October chill and strolled through a lake of cars reflecting an eerie orange glow pouring from the glass-fronted superstore. Friday. The place was packed.

He walked along a narrow path littered with broken glass and takeaway cartons, emerging onto a busy main road awash with Asian shops and restaurants. A heady scent of spice hung in the air while in the bustling gloom the street shimmered beneath a halo of neon; Ahmed's Cash and Carry, Barinda Curry House, Spicy Tandori Takeaway. His heart sank. He used to walk along this very street every morning with his friends on the way to primary school, laughing and joking past Alf's Newsagents, now an Halal butcher, past The Corner Cafe, now an Asian deli, past numerous other establishments that were once rock-solidly British; as British as

Britain was in the nineteen eighties. Another time. Another country.

He turned off the main road and headed down a scruffy side street of back-to-back terraces. A procession was taking place; fifty or so Asian men, teenage boys and toddlers — some wearing *thobes*, others in black puffer jackets worn over *sirwal* and *dishdasha* — were emerging from houses and walking along the street. Most were carrying copies of the Koran. Then Michael heard it; the trebly Arab proclamation booming over the rooftops; "*Allahu Akba. Allahu Akbar.*" It was the Friday Call to Prayer

As he turned the corner he saw the mosque; a plain Victorian red brick building with an Islamic facade of arched windows and a golden dome topped with a crescent moon. He realised it was the old Methodist chapel, the same chapel he attended every Sunday with his mother and father. Back then a small West Indian community used to gather — although his father never considered himself West Indian — resplendent in their Sunday best. But now a throng of Asian men greeted one another on the steps. Handshakes. Hugs. Kisses. Michael stopped, paralysed in thought. He saw the building as metaphor for what was happening to Britain.

"Hurry up, Brother. You'll miss the first prayer."

Michael turned to see an old Pakistani man with a deeply lined face framed by a wispy grey beard smiling up at him.

"I'm not going." he answered, emphatically.

Two teenagers butted in. "Then what are you doing round here? This is our area! Are you spying on us?"

The atmosphere was hostile.

"I'm visiting my granddad. He lives in the next street."

"Is he a Muslim?"

"What?"

"*La ilaha ilallah wa Muhammad ur-rusal ullah,*" proclaimed the loudspeaker.

"You heard!"

The old man nudged both teenagers. "Leave him alone. We'll be late for the first prayer." He raised his eyes as if to say, 'Young people these days! No manners.' He smiled apologetically before dragging the two boys off towards the mosque.

One of the teenagers looked back and muttered, "*Kafir!*"

Michael seethed. *You're the fucking infidel!* He cut down a back alley, his mind racing. *Our area! OUR area! Since when?* He emerged onto a darkened street. Looking up he saw the old familiar sign screwed to the wall: Clive Street, named as a tribute to Clive of India, although most West Indians back then used to joke it was named after the legendary cricketer Sir Clive Lloyd. He knew by heart that the next street was Victoria Street, home to his grandfather for over sixty years. And just on the corner was a place of childhood humiliation — Monroe's Newsagents — where, at the age of ten, he'd been caught stealing an Airfix model of a Spitfire. About to leave the shop mission accomplished Mrs Monroe had grabbed him by the collar and frogmarched him to his house three streets away. What happened when he got there was now a salty blur of tears, belt lashes and his mother's eternal shame. He would never steal again.

He shook off the memory and turned into Victoria Street. Munroe's Newsagents was now Narwaz Cash and Carry, a brightly-lit establishment spilling slanted trays of fruit and vegetables onto the street. The shop was crammed with goods of all descriptions, from plastic buckets to children's toys. *Sell anything these Asians. The next Jews.* Two women, invisible beneath black *burkas* and *nijabs,* were standing outside chatting. *How do they recognise each other?* They saw Michael and hunched closer together. He couldn't tell if they were smiling or scowling. *Imagine Emma putting up with that!*

His grandfather lived at number 22, half way down on the left. Twitching curtains accompanied his shadowy progress; 14-16-18. Finally he stood before the peeling green door. A host of memories flooded back; the day he stood on this very spot wearing his brand-new Cubs uniform; the time when, after a hectic journey down from Durham on the day his parents died, he collapsed into his grandfather's arms on the doorstep. Roots. Now he was the bringer of good news.

He knocked loudly, his heart racing. Two bolts and a chain eventually slid. The door inched opened.

"Yes?" A fragile black man in his nineties appeared, blinking. "Michael?" He looked him up and down for second, taking in his beautifully tailored clothes and handsome face. "Michael!" Come in, lad! Come in!" The accent was pure Mancunian.

He stepped inside and gave his paternal grandfather a hug. "Great to see you, Granddad. Really is." Michael's northern tones on the other hand had been softened by a first-class university education and years of Cotswold living.

"What's brought you here? I've not seen you in ages!"

Michael assuaged his guilt. "Not *that* long. You came to stay with us last year, remember? Emma and I took you to Blenheim Palace."

"Oh, yeah. So you did. It's been a while since you've been back in Levenshulme though, hasn't it?"

"Tell me about it."

"Anyway, come on through."

Michael walked into the lounge. As always it was sparsely furnished and fastidiously tidy — ancient three-piece suite, old-fashioned sideboard adorned with photos and knickknacks, TV, threadbare Turkish rug prostrate before a barely flickering gas fire.

"It's freezing in here, Granddad. Turn the fire up."

"The bills!"

Michael cranked up the fire two satisfying click, clicks. "Sod the bills." A gush of warmth emanated. He caught sight of a recently framed photo of King

Charles III hung on the wall next to one of the late Queen Elizabeth. And just below, perched on the sideboard where it had always been, the beloved black and white photograph of the man himself: Sergeant Rodwell Taylor, dressed in his army uniform standing beside a tank during the Korean War. Next to the photo, two gallantry medals were proudly displayed in their original case.

"How about a cuppa'?"

"Please, Granddad."

Michael followed Rodwell into the kitchen. He watched as his gnarled hands struggled with the cold water tap before shakily filling the kettle; the same hands that had pulled an injured colleague to safety during a firefight with Chinese troops at the Battle of Imjin River. The old man's skin was lighter than Michael's, his mother being white, whereas Michael's father had married a black woman, thus toning down a generation the myriad shades of the Taylor dynasty. Michael had married a white woman, just as his ancestor Bartholomew Francome Taylor had done back in the 19th century. The shade would again turn lighter when Michael's son Richard married his fiancé — the adorable Sophie, a recently qualified vet — and started his own family. There was rumoured to be Chinese somewhere in the Taylor gene pool. Michael, the family's genealogist, was on the hunt. But if, instead of trawling through page after page of dry records, he was to examine himself more closely in the mirror, he would have spotted it; the subtle

Oriental curve of his eyes, the slightly button nose.

It was his grandfather who first told him about Bartholomew; how, in 1838, a year after slavery was finally abolished in the Caribbean, he had signed up to work as a deckhand on a merchant ship bound for Liverpool. Michael was so taken with the story he rushed down to the local library and sought out *English Merchant Ships: 1800-1850*. Under the suspicious, bespectacled gaze of Miss Marsh, the chief librarian, he sat for over an hour staring at plate after plate of watercolours depicting clipper ships, brigs and schooners, captivated by their wooden hulls and billowing sails. One in particular caught his eye — the *RMS Trevelyan* — a three-masted, full rigged clipper that plied its trade between Liverpool and the Caribbean. Was this the very ship Bartholomew had sailed to England on? Walking back from the library he could only marvel at his ancestor's bravery.

"It's like Baghdad round here, Granddad. Bloody hell. I feel like a stranger in my own country."

Rodwell dropped a tea bag into each cup. "You can't stop progress."

"It's not as if they're patriotic. It's Islam this and Islam that. I bumped into two of them just now. They had the nerve to tell me it was their area. '*Their* area!'"

"They're not all like that. There's some lovely people round here."

"I'm not saying they are. Just the militant ones. I mean, imagine going to a Muslim country and pushing Christianity down their throat. You wouldn't last five minutes."

"Sugar?"

"No thanks. They're even trying to get Halal food served in Burford Primary School. Can you believe it!? In the heart of England! And there's only two Muslim kids there! Makes your blood boil."

Rodwell trudged wearily into the lounge, placed the tray on the sideboard and handed Michael a cup. "Sit down. I'm sure you didn't come here to talk about politics."

Michael's anger subsided. "No. I've got some news. Emma and I are moving back up north. We've bought a house in Wilmslow."

"Wilmslow! *Really!?*"

Michael smiled and nodded.

Rodwell couldn't contain his excitement. "It's only down the road! I'll be able to see you more often!"

"That's the idea."

"I'm thrilled, Michael. Thrilled! When are you moving in?"

"We exchanged contracts three weeks ago. So next weekend, all being well."

"So soon!"

"I didn't want to say anything in case it fell through."

"Wilmslow eh? Very posh… What about your job? Have you sorted something round here?"

"I've been offered the role of deputy head of

chambers at ITS Legal, one of the top law firms in Manchester. They do a lot of pro-bono work — free representation to people who can't afford to pay — which is what attracted me. They're based in the Royal Exchange building. So I'm slap bang in the heart of the city."

"Oh that's wonderful! Wonderful!" He struggled to his feet. "This call's for a celebration!" He opened the bottom drawer of the sideboard and produced a bottle of Bells.

"I thought the doctor had told you not to drink?"

"Bugger the doctor." He gripped the cap and twisted. "Damn!"

Michael was shocked to see how much his grandfather had aged since he last saw him; the once gentle giant had shrunk beyond all recognition.

"Don't strain yourself." Michael took the bottle and gave it a twist. "How's your heart?"

"Alright. Get a bit dizzy sometimes. Comes and goes."

Michael poured a tot into each cup.

Rodwell shook his head in amazement. "Deputy head of chambers, eh? Your dad would have been so proud."

"Not sure about that."

"Eh?"

"Cheers Granddad!"

They were about to drink a toast when a knock sounded at the door.

Rodwell froze.

"What's the matter?"

"Nothing!"

"Yes there is! Look at you!"

Michael walked into the hall and flung open the front door. Two *burka*-clad women stood motionless facing him.

"Bloody hell! You frightened the life out of me."

One of the women handed Michael a carrier bag full of shopping. "This is for Rodwell. He asked us to get a few things from the shop. His change is in the bag."

"Oh....Right...Thanks."

"Are you his grandson?" asked the second figure.

"Yes."

"Thought so. We noticed you earlier." They were the same women from outside Narwaz Cash and Carry. "He's always talking about you."

"Is he? That's nice." He stared into the narrow opening of the *nijab* and saw a pair of soft brown eyes upon him. He took the bag. "Thanks again for the shopping."

"Any time!"

He closed the door, walked back into the lounge and held up the bag. "Two women brought this."

The stress on Rodwell's face suddenly vanished. "Aleena and Haniya! Lovely girls. Can't do enough for me."

"Not for long." Michael put the bag down. "I've got some even better news... Emma and I want you to come and live with us. Not in the same house, you'll be pleased to know. We're looking to buy one of those retirement flats in Wilmslow. There's a block just around the corner. Emma noticed it when she first viewed the property. I say flats, they're luxury apartments… Wilmslow's a lovely area; safe streets, friendly people. You'll love it." He glanced at the gas fire. "And you *won't* have to worry about bills! I'll be able to see you every day, plus Emma said she'll do your shopping. Well, what do you think?"

Rodwell was touched by the offer; but what touched him most was his grandson's tender expression; the love in his eyes. Nevertheless he had to turn him down. "That's very generous of you, Michael, but your grandma and I, God rest her soul, scrimped and scraped to buy this house. We spent all our married life here. I'd feel like I was betraying her if I moved out. It's more than just bricks and mortar you know."

Michael felt as though he'd been punched in the stomach. He was desperate to make up for all the years he'd neglected his granddad. He'd kept in touch of course — a phone call once a month, presents every birthday and Christmas — but he'd never found the time to actually pay him visit; he was just too busy, preferring instead to pay his rail fare down to Oxford once every couple of years so he could spent the week in Burford. A lot easier that way.

"Grandma wouldn't think that. She'd be thrilled you were to going to live somewhere nice, with your family close by to take care of you. If she was here now she'd tell you."

"Sorry, lad. Your grandma died here and I intend to do the same."

Michael took a deep breath. "Look. Just think about it for a second. If you sell this place you'll have a nice little nest egg to do with as you ple—."

Rodwell exploded. "You sound like that bastard Khan! I will *not* be bullied into selling this house, no matter what the price! Understand!?" Straight away he realised he'd said something he shouldn't. But it was too late. Michael was on the case.

"Hold on. What Khan guy?"

Rodwell stared at the carpet. "No one. Forget it."

"No, no, no. You just said he's bullying you. Now who is he? I'm not leaving until you tell me."

Rodwell collapsed into the armchair. He realised it was useless trying to deceive his grandson — an experienced barrister able to outwit the most devious criminal — so why not tell him the truth, especially now he was moving back up north? Anyway, it would be relief; he'd kept it to himself long enough; endless nights lying awake in bed unable to sleep.

The bullying campaign began six months ago following an innocent knock at the front door. Rodwell opened it to find a smartly-dressed, middle-aged Asian man standing on the doorstep, a salesman's smile on his face. He introduced himself as Mr. Shoaib Khan, a local property developer. Apparently he was buying up the last remaining privately-owned houses in the area. He'd bought three houses on Victoria Street already. The owners were so delighted with his generous offer they immediately agreed to sell. Soon he'd own the whole street. So why not do the same? Rodwell thank him for his offer but politely refused. And that was that. Or so he thought.

Gradually, over the next few months, he was subject to an intimidation campaign — little things at first; kids knocking at the door and running away, mysterious taps on the front window in the evening. But each time Rodwell went to look there was no one there. Every few weeks a smiling Mr Khan would return, asking him if he'd changed his mind. Rodwell, getting more and more angry, ended up slamming the door in his face. When Aleena and Haniya next called round to pick up his shopping list he told them what had happened and asked if they knew who this Mr Khan was?

"Oh yes," said Haniya gravely. "We know him. He's our landlord. Always putting the rent up. Never does any repairs. Our roof has leaked for months. But we can do nothing. According to my husband he has links with organised crime. I'd be careful if I were you, Rodwell."

"I'm not frightened of him."

"Please!" begged Aleena. "Listen to Haniya. He's a powerful man. He always gets his way."

"Not in this case he won't!"

Frustrated that a stubborn old black man was

running his plans Khan cranked up the intimidation — dog shit was posted through letterbox, windows were broken. Then, after purchasing both houses either side of number 22, loud music and hammering came blasting through the walls at 3 a.m. Rodwell's nerves were shot to pieces. He thought about giving in, but every time Khan made an appearance at the front door, with his usual saccharine smile, Rodwell's pride got the better of him and he told him to piss off, slamming the door.

Blazing with anger Michael shot out of his chair. "Bloody hell Granddad! Why didn't *tell* me?!"

"I didn't want to worry you."

"A gangster's threatening you and you didn't want to *worry* me!" He paced the room. "Typical! They've only been in this country five minutes and —"

"Hey! That's enough! I won't have racist talk in this house!"

"It's not racist. It's fact!"

"It's bloody raci… Argg!" Rodwell clutched his chest, his face contorting in agony.

Michael rushed over and knelt down beside to him. "Granddad! Granddad!"

"G… Get my pills…In the drawer… over there. Second one down."

Michael hurried to the bureau and pulled open the drawer. He rooted around, found the bottle of pills, flipped open the lid and gave one to his granddad, who placed it under his tongue.

"I'll be… I'll be alright in a minute... Bloody angina."

"I'm sorry for stressing you out Granddad. We need to sort this out. I won't have you living like this."

"I'll decide what's best, Michael. Now if you don't mind I'd like to go to bed."

Michael helped Rodwell up the stairs and tucked him in. Before leaving he made his grandfather promise to phone him the next time Khan came to the house. "I'll come straight over. Now promise me."

Lying in bed Rodwell stared up at him, his frightened, skull-like features spot-lit by the bedside lamp. "I promise." He grasped Michael's hand shakily. "Thanks lad."

Tears welled up in his eyes. "You don't have to thank me, Granddad." He squeezed his hand. "Emma and I are moving in next weekend, so I'll see you then. And don't forget; phone me if you get any more threats… Night, night."

He closed the bedroom door, raging. *What kind of a coward threatens an old man!?* He left the house and made straight for Narwaz Cash and Carry in the hope of bumping into Aleena and Haniya; perhaps they could tell him more about this Khan character. When he got there he saw three women dressed in burka's standing outside. He couldn't tell if it was them or not, so carried on walking. Turning into the next street he saw the doors of the mosque open and a flood of Asian men come streaming out. Watching as they made their way home an intense hatred boiled up inside him.

III

Prime Minister Taylor strolled into the Audience Room. As requested by the king's private secretary he bowed, rising slowly to reveal a relaxed, friendly smile. "Honoured to meet you, your Majesty."

Briefed beforehand by the head of M15, the king was amazed at the new prime minister's body language; the way he walked into the room suggested someone with years of experience, not some political novice. But here he was, brimming with self- confidence.

As if to underline his determination to modernise the monarchy the king stepped forward and offered his hand. "William, please." They shook hands. "Good to meet you, Michael."

The handshake between the two men was warm, as was the eye contact, each putting the other at ease.

"May I say how sorry I am about your late father."

"Thank you." He gestured at one of two armchairs opposite the fireplace. "Do take a seat… Busy day?"

Michael sat. "Thank you… Very. My feet haven't touched the ground."

"Not surprising really. I mean, you're new to all this," said William, probing his new PM's apparent confidence and hinting at his lack of experience.

"As are you, if you don't mind me saying. Perhaps we can help each other?"

William smiled. "Yes, perhaps we can."

He brushed an imaginary speck of dust from his trousers. "As you've no doubt been told this is a formal meeting whereby the monarch gives their consent to the incoming government. But I *would* like to know more about how you intend to run the country. I've read your manifesto." Mindful of the monarch's role of not interfering in politics, he shifted awkwardly in his chair. "I have to say Michael it erm… it does seem rather erm…"

"Extreme?"

"Well, yes."

"If by extreme you mean rescuing our country from the insane asylum it has become, then yes, I suppose it is."

"But all this talk of deporting people; not exactly British is it."

"Only those who intend to do us harm: foreign criminals and religious agitators, and those who have no right whatsoever to be here." He wanted to use the assassination of the king's late father to make his point, but realised it would be insensitive. Instead he leaned forward, looking the king directly in the eye. "Can I ask you something, William? Would you allow a complete stranger to walk into your house without knowing who they were? Let them commit crimes without suffering the consequences? Allow them stay indefinitely for fear of being labeled a racist? Of course you wouldn't. No one in their right mind would. Yet that's exactly what this country's been doing for the past however many decades. It's hardly surprising then that ordinary, law-abiding citizens — the silent majority who built this great nation of ours, let's not forget — are sick to the back teeth of the situation, especially when foreign criminals are unable to be deported. As of today GB Patriots are putting a stop to that. Along with a much stricter immigration policy — more on the lines of the Australian points system, whereby we will only allow people to settle in the UK who actually benefit the country and embrace our values, rather than the other way around — we intend to completely dismantle the current system and replace it with one that actually works, removing people swiftly and efficiently without the interference of immigration lawyers."

William looked at him nervously. "So my government is actually pulling out of the European Convention on Human Rights?"

"Absolutely. For too long this outmoded legislation has been used to protect the rights of criminals who wish to do us harm. In my opinion it's completely irrelevant in modern-day Britain. If we want to remove someone we shouldn't have to go cap-in-hand to some court in Strasburg. We should do it ourselves; which is why my party has just been elected with a massive majority, despite being labeled racist and extremist by the political left, who, deep down, hate what this country stands for."

William picked up a copy of GB Patriots manifesto. "But all this talk of," he opened it and read the first page, "'purging society of negative elements.' What does that mean exactly?"

"It means that for too long certain institutions — so called 'trusted institutions' like our major broadcasters and education system — have been doing their level best to undermine this country. Why that is, is beyond me. I mean, to me this is the finest country in the world. But no, all we hear about is how unfair we are, and how racist our society is. Which begs the question, if that's the case, why do so many people from all corners of the globe want to come here? And once they are here, instead of expecting them to conform to our way of life, these so-call 'trusted institutions' tell them the exact opposite; to stick to their own culture whilst undermining ours in the process."

He threw up his hands, "It makes no sense. No sense at all… One thing's for sure, William, Britain certainly wasn't like that when *I* was growing up."

IV

MICHAEL'S CHILDHOOD was crystal clear, his sharp legal mind able to recall events in precise detail. After leaving Levenshulme Primary he won a scholarship to one of the most prestigious Grammar schools in the area. The day the confirmation letter arrived at the house, addressed to his father, Joel, Michael was in his bedroom gluing together the fuselage of a Wellington Bomber. He was just about to drop the rear-gunner into place — a tricky job that required all his concentration — when suddenly his father's stern voice called out…

"Michael. Come down here."

He froze. *What have a done!* He put the Wellington on the bed and walked slowly down the stairs. Approaching the living room door he swallowed hard (his father believed in old-fashioned discipline, the memory of the Monroe's corner shop incident the previous year still fresh in his mind). He needn't have worried. The moment he opened the door and saw the look of pride on his mother's face as she held out the letter he knew he'd won the scholarship. After an avalanche of hugs and kisses an impromptu party was held. Soon the house was filled with friends and relatives. Even the old Irish lady from across the street turned up, peppering his face with gummy kisses. Rodwell was the last to arrive. Enveloping Michael in a bear hug he told everyone in the room how proud he was of his talented grandson. "A future prime minister!" he boasted.

"I'll be happy if he finds a job," laughed Joel. "We could do with the money."

That first day; it was as if someone had dropped him into another world. The whole ethos of the school, its focus on academic subjects balanced with a varied sports program, fitted him like a glove. It didn't take long before he was accepted, his good-looks and quick mind in the debating society winning people over. There were the usual racial slurs of course; he was used to that from primary school. But here they were more subtle. Because he associated with the conservative element in the school — serious pupils who studied hard and wanted to get on in life — Michael attracted the ire of two factions; the arty left-wing crowd who wanted to tear down the establishment, and the Asian pupils who viewed him as an interloper. The arty faction, disappointed he hadn't flocked to their anti-establishment banner as they had assumed he would, turned on him, accusing him of being a 'traitor to his race.' Michael laughed, telling them that as far as he was aware he belonged to the Human Race. With the Asian pupils it was more a case of 'know your place.' "This is how things work in this country, Taylor," said one; the son of a multi-millionaire clothing entrepreneur from Hale Barns, "Whites first, Asians second, Blacks third." Michael's response was to ask his inquisitor when his family had first come to the UK. "Just after the Second World War," he boasted. Michael pointed out that his ancestors had arrived in the early 19th century. Beat that! He relished the hypocrisy. All his life he'd been taught by his mother never to judge someone by the colour of their skin, and now here he was, being judged by the very people who were guilty of the exact same racism they purported to detest. You couldn't make it up.

His character was formed during these fractious encounters, shaping him into a person with a keen sense of justice, someone who refused to let race define him, however difficult that was — and at times, as a black person growing up, it was extremely difficult — but he always gave it his best shot.

Michael's closest friend at school was a boy called Tom Hampshire. They first got to know one another in Year 9 when they were selected for the cricket team. Despite Tom running him out in the very first game of the season they instantly bonded. The son of a wealthy accountant from Bowdon, Tom was a serious boy with a wicked sense of humour. You could never tell if he was joking, which Michael found fascinating. Tom was drawn to Michael's open, friendly character, his adventurous, try-anything-once attitude. He was one of the best connected boys in the school, and introduced him to his large circle of friends. A smaller group soon coalesced around Michael — Tom, Giles, a maths prodigy from Wilmslow, and Harry, a politics nut from Bramhall. All three came from wealthy, upper middle class families.

It was at a barbecue at Tom's house during his third term that Michael met his first serious girlfriend; a languid, beguiling blonde from Mottram St. Andrew. Sadie was sixteen and went to Alderley Edge High School for Girls. The moment he set eyes on her, he was hooked. Aside from the fact she resembled a young Vanessa Paradis, it was her utter confidence that bowled him over; a confidence born of a cast-iron certainty that one day she would marry a multi-millionaire who would cherish and take care of her. Not for Sadie the stress of finding a job and struggling with a mortgage. You only had to look at her floating round the Hampshire's back garden — the centre of attention to all her female friends, the sexual fantasy of every man present — to know she would get her wish. But all that would come later. Now she wanted to have fun, to test-drive the wonderful gift Nature had given her. And what better way of satisfying her rebellious streak than to date a handsome black boy — white boys were so last week.

Sadie's gene pool, Michael would soon discover, included a fabulously wealthy father — a chubby, bucktoothed hedge fund manager from Bath called David — and her mother Caroline, a glamorous, ex-fashion-model. Common sense suggested their offspring would be marred by David's physical drawbacks. But no. Nature had surprised everyone by combining Caroline's willowy frame with David's piercing blue eyes to produce a strawberry-blonde of perfect proportions, his buck teeth toned down into a maddeningly sexy pout that gave the impression of constant sexual arousal. Standing beneath a stripy blue awning shading the makeshift bar, she eyed Michael's athletic frame greedily from across the patio.

Tom nudged him. "You've copped."

Michael was too busy taking in his dreamy surroundings — the five-bedroom detached house, the immaculate lawns, the relaxed, cosy nature of the all-white crowd peppered with the odd Indian and Chinese couple. Before leaving for the barbecue Michael's father had told him not to stand for any racist nonsense. But the Hampshire's and their friends couldn't have been more welcoming.

"Michael!"

"What?"

"Sadie keeps staring at you!"

"Who?"

Michael followed the direction of Tom's sidelong glance. He was stunned to see a heavenly vision looking at him, a wilful expression on her face.

"She goes to my sister's school. She's red h— What are you doing?

Without thinking Michael had put his glass of Coke down and marched towards her across the patio, surprising even himself. As he approached he noticed a look of triumph dawn on her face.

"Hi, I'm—"

She grabbed his hand. "I know. Let's get out of here.

Sadie made off with her latest acquisition, snatching a bottle of Blue Nun off the kitchen table before leading him out through the front door

"Let's drink this in Dunham Park," she said, pointing down a long tree-lined road bathed in evening sunshine. "It's down there... I'm Sadie by the way."

Walking beside her past huge Edwardian mansions nestling discreetly within beautifully manicured gardens, Michael thought he'd died and gone to heaven. What could be more perfect than this? He thought about Clive Street and Victoria Street, their pokey back-to-back terraces. This was the real England; the England buried deep inside him; the England he knew so well yet had never once visited. For the first time in his life he felt connected.

"Hold this."

Sadie handed him the wine, jumped over a stile and ran off laughing into the park, scattering the deer.

"Wait for me!" Michael followed, chasing after her.

Eventually she ran out of breath and slumped down, resting against the trunk of an ancient lime tree. She patted the ground next to her, inviting him to sit.

Michael obliged. Breathless, he stared in awe at the undulating parkland, its ankle-deep grass and clumps of lace-like ferns dwarfed by mature oaks, beeches and limes. In the distance, to his right, he could see part of a huge stately home.

"What's that place?"

"Dunham Hall."

His love of history kicked in, sending his thoughts into overdrive. "Oh wow! Imagine being born in a place like that, with butlers and maids looking after you."

Sadie grinned, shaking her head. "You're funny."

"When was it built, d'you know?"

"Who gives a fuck. Open the wine and let's get shitfaced."

There was a problem; in their rush to leave the Hampshire's they had forgotten to nab a corkscrew.

"Oh my God! Disaster!" said Sadie, over-dramatically. "I know! Smash the neck against the tree."

"You must be joking. We'll get glass in the wine. I've got a better idea."

He stood up and snapped off a narrow, low-hanging branch. Peeling off the foil he took the end of the branch, placed it in the centre of the cork and slammed it against the trunk. After three attempts the cork vanished inside the bottle.

"No way!" cried Sadie. "Fit and practical!" She took the bottle and gulped down three good mouthfuls. "Cheap shit, but it'll do." She handed him the wine. "Go for it."

Michael's only experience of alcohol was sharing

a can of Woodpecker cider with Tom one afternoon after cricket practice. He didn't particularly like the effect, unlike Tom, who revelled in the fuzzy, floating sensation. But here he was, being offered it by the girl of his dreams. He took the bottle, closed his eyes and swallowed the tepid liebfraumilch. Uggh! It was worth it. In the warm, humid evening, as dusk fell over the park, they relaxed and began to chat. Michael told her all about Levenshulme, about his mum and dad, his granddad and the history of his family.

Then it was Sadie's turn.

"Dad made shitloads of money on the stock market. That's where he met Mum, at some swanky party in the City. They relocated to Cheshire before I was born. He's got an office in Manchester now with loads of people working for him."

"What does your mum do?"

"What do you mean, what does she do?"

"For a job?"

"A job! Oh my God you must be joking! Mummy doesn't work. All she does is spend Dad's money." She grinned. "Actually that is her job" She took another swig of wine. "She's always redecorating the house. You'll have to come over before she changes it. Again! They'd love to meet you."

"Great."

"And I wanna meet your mum and dad."

Michael cringed at the thought of taking Sadie to Levenshulme.

"OK," he said, reluctantly.

"You know what this means, don't you?"

"What?"

"It means we're dating." She snuggled up close, resting her head on his shoulder.

A strange aroma rose up to greet him; one he'd never encountered before: rich, white, nubile flesh. He felt himself getting hard.

Tilting her head she looked into his eyes. "Kiss me… I've always wanted to be kissed by a black boy."

If Michael had been impressed with the Hampshire's place, the Hudson residence blew his mind. Set in fifteen acres of pristine Cheshire countryside, the mini estate boasted an outdoor heated swimming pool, two tennis courts, a traditional Swedish sauna, a four-car air-conditioned garage, and an ultra-modern steel and glass annex her father used as an office. The pure white Georgian mansion seemed to shimmer, Michael recalled on his first visit, like a longed-for oasis in the desert.

Holding hands with Sadie in the back of her mother's Range Rover as it cruised up the drive, the moment he saw the house his whole body went tense. He tried to look cool, but the triumphant glint in Caroline's eyes in the rear-view mirror told him he hadn't succeeded. She loved bringing new people to the house and watching them squirm, or, in the case of her daughter's new boyfriend, stare with a kind of blank terror.

When Caroline opened the front door and led him into the hall, with its black and white checkerboard floor, marble pillars and stucco ceiling, he went all light-headed. Only Hollywood movie stars live like this!

"Take Michael into the kitchen would you darling and get yourselves a drink."

"Yes Mummy."

"Lovely to meet you, Michael."

"And you, Mrs Hudson… And thank you for picking me up."

"Oh my God!" cried Sadie. "Stop being so polite!"

"Take no notice of her Michael. It's nice to have good manners… Makes a change from the usual louts she brings round," Caroline smiled, "See you at lunch," before gliding up the double staircase.

"Your mum's beautiful," he said.

Sadie dug her elbow into the ribs. "Hey!"

"Not as beautiful as you, obviously."

She kissed him on the cheek. "Obviously!"

The kitchen was vast, with aluminium cupboards surrounding a black marble central worktop. The latest stainless steel gadgets stood to attention in various corners, while hidden behind smoked glass, the temperature monitored by flickering LEDs, bottles of vintage wine lay slumbering on their sides.

"It's like the Starship Enterprise," was his gobsmacked reaction.

"You're funny," giggled Sadie. She opened the

huge Smeg refrigerator and peered inside. "Coke OK?"

Light streamed in through a set of French windows to his right, pulling his gaze out towards rolling fields dotted with sheep."

"Michael!"

"Sorry! Coke's fine… Are they your sheep?"

"What?... Oh yeah. Dad bought them for a laugh." She handed him a perfectly chilled bottle of Coke. "Come on. I wanna show you my bedroom."

"Can I see the rest of the house first?"

"What for?"

"It's not every day I come to a place like this."

"Oh come on then!"

She hurried him through a series of reception rooms, each one immaculately presented and filled with expensive furnishings.

Michael was stunned. "It's like a show house."

"That's the problem."

Walking back into the hall they climbed the curving staircase, turned left and headed down a wide landing covered in beige shag pile. Sadie's bedroom was four times the size of his and looked out over the swimming pool. After rushing to the window to take in the view, he turned to see a queen-size bed piled with cuddly toys, a mirrored dressing table crammed beauty products, a walk-in wardrobe, and an en-suite bathroom; a gap in the partially-open door revealing a slice of pink marble topped with a gold tap. Above the bed a crystal chandelier caught the afternoon light.

He shook his head. "Unreal."

"I'll show you what's unreal." She slid the straps of her summer dress off her shoulders and let it fall to the ground.

"What do you want to do with your life, Michael?" asked David, beating time with his index finger on the clear glass dining table while staring off into the garden.

"I want to be a lawyer."

Diverted from thinking about shorting the shares of a well-known global bank, David blinked.

"A lawyer!?"

Michael was enjoying a delicious, getting-to-know-you lunch in the Hudson's minimalist dining room. David was dressed like an art-house film director — baggy black Yamamoto trousers, black sweatshirt, black flip-flops, his exhausted puffy face proof of a morning spent glued to a multiplex of financial screens. Caroline, on the other hand, fresh from the sauna, looked radiant in her pink Juice tracksuit, her flawless skin glowing.

"A defence lawyer."

"A *defence* lawyer!" David mulled it over, nodding. "Well good for you, Michael. Says a lot about a person that.

"Your parents must be proud of you," added Caroline, topping up her Riesling.

His mother was, deeply. As for his father, he

wasn't so sure. Recently they had begun to argue; Michael's slow drift into adulthood threatening Joel's masculinity. Pride in his son for attending one of the best grammar schools in the country had now curdled into seething jealousy, fuelled by the effortless way Michael breezed through each of his exams. It's not like he wanted him to fail exactly, but at least he wanted him to struggle. Then he could have his late-night father and son moment — "Listen Michael. I'm here for you. I believe in you one hundred per cent. You're a gifted boy, so get your head down and do your best. I'll always be here for you, no matter what." Denied that paternal input Joel felt he was losing his son to a world where he no longer mattered. Mealtimes were the worst. The dinner table had become a battle ground, a place where Michael's newfound ideas were shot down in flames, especially his nascent political views — his free-market Thatcherite leanings influenced by his upper middle-class school friends.

"You don't know what you're talking about, boy!" Joel would scream, banging the table. "That bitch ruined this country! She forced millions of hard-working people into poverty! So keep your mouth shut in future!"

It always ended in the same way, with his mother rushing out of the kitchen in tears. Yet still his father hadn't finished. "Now see what you've done… upsetting your mother like that," he'd shout, and the rest of the meal was eaten in silence. As for Michael's burning desire to be lawyer, he decided to keep it himself, certain his father would only laugh in his face.

So to be in the company of the Hudsons, a family who were open to all sorts of ideas and opinions, well, that was liberating.

"Sadie tells me you're taking her to meet your parents next week," said Caroline.

"Err, yeah. Yes I am," answered Michael nervously.

I'm SO not looking forward to that!

"For some of your mother's home cooking I believe?"

"That's right. Mum's a great cook."

"Sadie *loves* Caribbean food, don't you, darling?" Sadie nodded.

"Oh Mum doesn't cook Caribbean food. Dad doesn't like it. We only eat English food."

"Really?"

The night before Sadie's visit Michael was so stressed he barely slept. Lying in bed the next morning listening to his mother preparing breakfast, all sorts of scenarios went through his head: Sadie taking one look at the house and rushing back home; his father ignoring her because of what she represented; or worst, insulting her, calling her a pampered Cheshire princess who didn't have a day's work in her, which was true. But it was his mother's reaction Michael feared most.

Doreen was a kind, modest lady who saw the good in everyone; the complete opposite of her husband Joel, a born cynic. They had got together in 1981 after meeting at Pips nightclub in Manchester. Joel was an apprentice plasterer at the time, while Doreen worked as a check-out girl at a Tesco's in Stretford. Joel was drawn to Doreen's dark, mysterious beauty, the modest way she held herself. Doreen on the other hand was attracted to Joel's ambitious nature; the night they met he told her he was planning to start his own plastering business...

"A whole fleet of vans covering the northwest, with 'Taylor Plastering Service' written on the side. This isn't fantasy, Doreen. I'm gonna make it happen."

They were married in 1984 and found a council house to rent in Levenshulme, three streets away from Rodwell. Two years later Michael was born; their only child. Sadly, due to the recession of the early 80s, the plastering business never materialised, and Joel was forced to take whatever menial job was on offer. A terrible sense of failure had haunted him ever since, leaving him with a deep hatred of the rich.

Unlike most of the powerful West Indian matriarchs who lived close by, Doreen was happy to take a back seat, leaving the running of the family to Joel. Her gentle acquiescence sometimes slid into a grating subservience, especially when it came to dealing with white people in authority. Michael remembered one painful episode in particular. He was six-years-old when a petty council official called at the house to discuss the thorny issue of the rent — apparently Joel, who was out looking for work at the time, had written to the council asking if they qualified for a rent reduction. The official, a thin, nasty man with a bald head and the face of a stoat, called round unannounced and proceed to give his mother a lecture.

"Oh don't bother putting the kettle on, Mrs Taylor. This won't take long. First of all, your husband has got some nerve writing to the council. You people have no idea of the struggle previous generations went through to allow you the luxury of living in a council house. And here you are, you've only been in this country five minutes, asking for a reduction in the rent! It beggars belief, it really does. Now you'll pay the same rent as everyone else or you'll be evicted! Is that clear?"

Instead of shoving him up against the wall and reeling off the list of Taylor's who had fought and died for Britain in countless wars — from the Crimean to the Korean — like Joel would have done, Michael watched as his mother went to pieces, saying how very sorry she was, pleading with him not to take the matter further, that she was extremely grateful to the council, and that yes, of course, they would continue to pay the same rent as everyone else.

When he'd gone Doreen sat Michael down and made him promise not tell his father what had happened. Michael kept his word, which was why he was so worried about Sadie coming over. God knows how she would react when the self-entitled white princess arrived.

But it never happened. After a long wait at the prearranged meeting point Sadie failed to turn up. Worried she'd been involved in an accident he ran to the nearest phone box and called her house in Mottram St Andrew. Caroline answered. After a short pause, in which angry, muffled voices could be heard, Sadie came on the line.

"Hello?"

"Sadie! Oh thank God you're alright. Are you still com—"

"I'm sorry Michael.

"W… what do you mean, you're sorry? Mum's prepared food. She's gone to a lot of trou—"

"It's over."

Suddenly the line went dead. He stood there in complete shock, the sound of the traffic roaring in his ears. He slowly replaced the receiver. Pain; he'd never felt anything like it. He trudged back home, memories of the night in Dunham Park racing through his mind; the smell of her hair, the taste of her lips, the utter loveliness of her being. As he approached Munroe's newsagents he lost control. He ran down a side alley and collapsed sobbing against the wall.

Worse was to come when he got home. Trying to keep his emotions in check he pushed open the front door.

"At last!" shouted his mother. "Well, bring her through."

He walked into the living room. There were his parents, standing to attention in their Sunday best — Doreen in a green satin dress with a butterfly collar, her long hair piled up in a bun, Joel wearing the dark blue suit he wore to church. Next to them was a side table groaning with fancy cakes and freshly-made sandwiches, a wisp of steam rising from the spout of Doreen's best Royal Albert tea pot. Both were smiling expectantly. Michael took one look at his mother's face and broke down. "She's… she's not coming," he stammered, and ran up the stairs.

Half way to the top he heard his father's voice. "I knew it."

Michael crashed onto the bed and buried his face in the pillow, vowing never again to fall in love. He did of course, many times, though not as deeply as he had with Sadie. Years would go by before he felt the same way about someone — his future wife Emma.

Despite the pain of his adolescent affair, it had ingrained in him a certain type he would never stray from — slim, blonde, blue-eyed white girls.

Girls, however, were very much off the agenda for the time being; he had his A-levels to contend with.

After weeks of cramming he took his exams. Waiting for the results was purgatory. Finally an official-looking letter arrived at the house. He ran upstairs and tore it open — six A*.

V

BATHED IN RED, white and blue, Wembley Stadium blazed beneath the evening sky. Inside, searchlights criss-crossed the arena as a flotilla of drones in the shape of a golden acorn hovered above a huge stage decked out in Union Jacks. For the past two hours the packed stadium had been entertained by the cream of British popular music; a diverse range of artists from rap stars to rock musicians to classical virtuosos. Some had refused to perform due to their political beliefs, but the majority were there, keen to boost album sales and to prove to their fans they were right behind the country's charismatic new leader. One legendary rock singer, known in the past for his outspoken left-wing views, even went so far as to announce that it was about time Britain had elected someone who put the country first. "The killing of our king was a line in the sand for me, man."

Free at last from the constraints of political correctness the crowd roared its approval. Quick to exploit the fervent, patriotic atmosphere, each of the performers tried to outdo the other in their eulogising of the mother country, one notorious rap artist leading the crowd in a Grime version of 'Rule Britannia'.

At 9pm precisely the stadium was plunged into darkness. Quietly, unnoticed at first, the sound of a lone violin playing the strains of 'Land of Hope and Glory' drifted through the PA system. Gradually the volume increased and the tension began to mount. As the crowd became more and more excited the strings joined in. Then the brass added its weight to the glorious, heartrending anthem, whipping the audience into a frenzy as they sang as one — young, old, black, white, Asian, people from all corners of the Commonwealth in fact — "Land of Hope and Glory, Mother of the free," while high above the stadium the drones reformed into the shape of the Union flag.

An unseen announcer proclaimed, "Ladies and gentlemen, our *new* Prime Minister!"

Suddenly a powerful spotlight illuminated the centre of the stage. There, standing on a dais wearing an immaculately-tailored black suit, white shirt and pencil-thin black tie, was Prime Minister Michael Taylor, arms outstretched encompassing the whole of Wembley Stadium. The crowd erupted. Basking in the applause his smiling face was projected onto huge screens above the stage, the whole captivating drama beamed into every household in the UK and newsfeeds around the globe. Eventually the crowd quietened and the prime minister began to speak, softly at first…

"I want to read a quote from the great Roman statesman Cicero, 'You provide here, citizens, a road to fame which has always been wide open to every man of merit, and yet to me it has been barred.'

"People of Great Britain, by casting your vote at the ballot box you have caused a political earthquake, the likes of which will be felt for generations to come. A profound change has taken place in this country, and I stand before you now as proof of that change. As your leader I won't make empty promises or engage in fancy political rhetoric. I vow at all times to speak to you in a plain, straightforward manner. So let me say this to each and every one of you in the language of the common man; we live in the greatest country in the world, the birthplace of free speech and freedom of expression, the land of free-thinkers and libertarianism. In short, the envy of the world. Sadly, as you all know, over the years this inherent right has been hijacked by the twisted, brainwashing policies of the Left; policies so insidious that people have actually been afraid to speak their minds, the right of every Briton since time immemorial. Well no more! Tonight I'm proud to say this; that after years of political mismanagement and misguided social engineering, we have finally won our country back."

VI

MICHAEL FIRST GOT into politics during his second year at Durham University. As part of his law degree he was encouraged to join the debating society: fierce, passionate debate would hone his cross-examining skills when he became a barrister. Being one of the top debaters at his old school he soon gained a reputation for ruthless questioning and the merciless dismantling of opponents. He loved the cut and thrust of the whole affair, likening it to gladiatorial combat. But it was during political debates that he excelled, especially when it came to left versus right-wing issues. As with most debating societies you were told beforehand which side you represented and argued your point. For instance, when the motion 'Thatcher's Policy To Close The Coalmines Was a Good Thing' was debated, Michael represented the left, arguing that the decision had been calamitous for British Industry. Such was his charisma and all-round debating skills he won the debate hands down, leaving his opponent floundering. Later, in the bar, he was approached by a scruffy white guy in his early thirties wearing a black trench coat and red scarf. He told him he was member of the Socialist Workers Party and that he was impressed with his communicative skills and intimate knowledge of the facts.

"We could do with someone like you in the party.

Fancy joining the cause?"

Flattered, he politely told him no; his views were already formed; he was a die-hard Conservative.

The man stared at him, flabbergasted. "*You vote Tory*!? *A black guy*!"

Michael looked him in the eye. "Can I ask you something? Would you have asked me that if I was white?"

He froze; nowhere in the SWP's recruitment manual was there a subsection on dealing with black Conservatives. As far as the SWP were concerned they simply didn't exist.

"Erm… I erm…"

"Exactly. Have a good night."

He came across this racial stereotyping more and more at university. After a while he began to enjoy it. The look on people's faces, black as well as white, when he expressed his political views said a lot about British society.

After dipping his toe in the water via the debating society he decided to go the whole hog and join Durham Young Conservatives, popping along to their head office one evening. Once again he was surprised by the reaction of the members, especially chairman, who was both 'thrilled and surprised' by his application.

But the real eye-opener came when he was out canvassing during the 2003 local elections sporting a blue rosette. This was Blair country, the prime minister's constituency of Sedgefield right next door.

Labour was riding high in the polls, so he knew he'd have his work cut out. But it wasn't local issues that dominated the doorstep conversation. It was the fact he was a black Conservative. At the time all the newly-elected black MPs represented the Labour Party — Diane Abbot, Bernie Grant, Paul Boateng — so what on earth was he doing supporting the Tories? Some houses he called at were downright racist. One staunch Labourite, a retired coal miner, told him he was betraying his people and that he should be ashamed of himself. At another, a black bus driver called him a coconut before telling him to told fuck off. He tried steering the conversation away from race to local issues like housing and transport, but the majority of people just stared at him with condescending smirks. Tired and frustrated he gave up politics and concentrated on finishing his law degree.

During his third year at Durham Michael received news that would change his life. He was in the library studying for his finals when he was approached by the Student Welfare Officer, a physics undergraduate called Penny.

"Would you come to the office please, Michael. You have an urgent phone call."

"Who is it? Can't it wait?"

"You need to come now!"

He could tell by the look on Penny's face it was serious. So he got up and followed her to the bursar's office.

"Hello?"

It was an Inspector from Greater Manchester Police. There was no easy way of putting this; his parents had been killed in a road accident. Michael dropped the phone and fell to the floor. Eventually Penny helped him to his feet, sat him down and gave him a glass of brandy. After that everything was a blur. He half recalled dashing to the station and boarding the next train to Manchester. From there he must have caught a taxi to Levenshulme, because the next thing he remembered was collapsing in his grandfather's arms.

Rodwell took him into the kitchen, sat him down and told him what had happened. Apparently his parents were in sitting the back of a taxi travelling into Manchester along Princess Parkway when an articulated lorry lost control and ploughed into them.

"According to the police the truck was on the other side of the road when the driver had a heart attack. He must have veered across and… The people in the car behind were killed as well… What a tragic waste of life."

"What were they doing going into Manchester?" asked Michael, hoping to bury his emotions under an avalanche of mundane facts.

"I don't know… Maybe your mother wanted to go shopping."

"But why did Dad go? He hates shopping."

Concerned, Rodwell looked at his grandson; he was staring at the check tablecloth, his eyes on stalks.

He reached across and squeezed his hand.

"I don't know, Michael. Why does anyone do anything?"

It was as if a dam had been breached. Michael lowered his head and burst into tears. Rodwell got up, moved quickly around the table and held him as he sobbed his heart out.

The funeral was held at Southern Cemetery, a short distance away in Chorlton-Cum-Hardy. Generations of Taylors had been laid to rest there, which was a great comfort to Michael. He stayed with Rodwell for a couple of days then headed back to Durham; with only weeks to go before his finals he needed to get his head down and study.

Most people would have found that impossible. The opposite was true of Michael. Perhaps it was because, as an only child with little or no support, he realised it was up to him to make his way in the world and that no one else would help him. Whatever the reason, it revealed a cold, hard logic. As one of his tutors remarked to a colleague one day in the Common Room, "That Taylor boy will go far."

After graduating with an honours degree he immediately applied to one of the Inns of Court to begin his legal training — a two-year process which ended in being Called to the Bar. Because of his financial situation he was accepted on a scholarship by the prestigious Middle Temple. Unlike most of his fellow students, who decided to take a gap year and see the world, Michael moved straight down to

London. Travel was the last thing on his mind. He was determined to be one step ahead of everyone else.

He found a cheap flat to rent in Elephant and Castle using some of the money his parents had left him in their will as a deposit. To fund his day-to-day expenses he took a succession of part-time jobs — barman, waiter, delivery driver. The run-down area was an odd mix of poor immigrant families and even poorer artists. He must have cut a strange figure walking to the station each morning dressed in his new suit. But that was nothing compared to the culture shock he experienced when he arrived at Middle Temple, mixing with fellow students and barristers among the historic and richly decorated medieval buildings. He didn't realise how historic until he discovered Temple Church and saw the stone effigies of the Knight Templars, an order of religious knights founded in Jerusalem in 1119 to defend the pilgrimage routes after the fall of Fatimid Caliphate. He became obsessed with their history, reading anything he could lay his hands on. What especially fascinated him were the many battles fought by the Crusaders, such as the Battle of Arsuf in 1191, where a multi-national force led by King Richard I of England — which included a sprinkling of African Knights from the Ethiopian Church — defeated the armies of the Ayyubid Sultanate led by Saladin.

Often, when he wanted some peace and quiet,

he would enter Temple Church and stare at the long-dead knights lying beneath its Romanesque dome. Studying each one in detail he recalled the famous legend predicting that, should England ever come under attack, these same knights would rise up to defend her.

Two years later he was Called to the Bar and began his pupillage at one of London's leading criminal barrister's chambers. He trained under Sir Graham Dowling QC, assisting him in two major trails, one of which — defending a woman accused of murdering her husband — was held at the Old Bailey. The first time he entered the legendary Court Number One, scene of some of the most famous trails in British history, Michael knew he'd chosen the right profession.

One night he was in a pub close to his chambers celebrating the birthday of a senior clerk when he spotted an attractive, vivacious blonde playing pool. Intrigued, he wandered over and started chatting. Her name was Emma. She told him she was in her final year at Kings studying medicine and that after graduating she was heading to the John Radcliffe Hospital in Oxford to work as a junior doctor. "I'm from Woodstock. I'm fed up of living in London so I want to move back home." When Michael told her he was training to be a barrister she was shocked. "Really?! You don't seem the legal type."

"Why not?"

"I don't know. We've only just met, but you seem

more happy-go-lucky." She smirked and pointed over towards his colleagues. "Unlike those stuffed shirts over there."

Michael laughed. "Those 'stuffed shirts' happen to be some of the finest legal minds in Britain. But thanks for the compliment."

As soon as they started dating it was obvious they were made for each other. At the end of the year Michael qualified as a barrister. Finding a job was a breeze. Inundated with offers from London-based law firms keen to cherry-pick the latest talent, nevertheless he chose instead to work for Tyler, Watt & Harris, an ancient law firm based in Oxford. What swung it for Michael, apart from the fact that Emma was about to relocate there, was the company letterhead — Tyler, Watt & Harris. Est. 1838 — the exact same year his ancestor Bartholomew Francome Taylor had first come to England from the West Indies.

VII

SADIE TOOK HIS HAND, her blue eyes sparking. "Oh my God, Michael. I… I don't know what to say. That was amazing. Absolutely amazing." She snuggled up close as the blacked-out Range Rover flanked by police motorcycles headed through central London towards Downing Street. "Look at all the people!"

Michael glanced through the tinted glass at the cheering crowds thronging the streets. Fresh from his victory speech at Wembley Stadium he'd never felt so alive, so absolutely sure that what he was doing was right.

The secure telephone inside the car rang. His press officer came on the line. "The President of the United States, Prime Minister."

"Put her on…. Madam President! How are you?.. You watched my speech!? I'm flattered… Thank you… Thank you. I appreciate your support… Yes, I'm looking forward to working you too. I'm sure we'll do great things together… Absolutely! See you in Washington next week."

Michael lifted Sadie's hand and planted a kiss on the engagement ring he'd given her a few weeks before the election; her glamorous presence boosting his popularity in the polls and guaranteeing countless photo opportunities. She had come back into his life following his divorce from Emma, bumping into him one night during a fundraising dinner at the Midland Hotel in Manchester. She was with her father David, one of the biggest contributors to GB Patriots, whose generosity had earned him a seat at Michael's table. When Michael entered the room and sat down, Sadie was sitting right opposite. It was as if time had stood still and he was back in Dunham Park all those years ago. She hadn't changed a bit — the same languid smile and carefree attitude, the same brash confidence. If anything she was more beautiful. Recently divorced from her second husband, a wealthy Parisian banker, Sadie had moved back to the UK and was now living in a penthouse apartment in Alderley Edge. So when her father told her he'd been invited to the fundraiser, she insisted on coming along. As soon as Michael set eyes on her he knew that fate had brought them together.

After the dinner was over Michael invited David and Sadie to join him for drink in the hotel bar. David strategically refused. "You two go ahead. I'm sure you've got a lot of catching up to do… And Michael, that day you came for lunch, I had a feeling you'd go far."

Michael ordered a round of drinks and they found a quite table.

"I never took you for a politician," she said, playing with the slice of lemon in her gin and tonic, angling to see if he still had feelings for her. "I thought you were too nice."

"Is that why you dumped me?"

Oh yes, he still liked her alright; she could tell by the hurt on his face. She nudged him playfully. "Oh Michael, that's so unfair. I was a baby. I had no idea what I wanted."

"You do now, I suppose."

That was forward of him. "So do you, by what you said in your speech. Dad was *really* impressed. Mind you, he's always been a closet patriot. Do you know what he said to me in the car on the way here? He said he was amazed that an unknown black guy had managed to awaken something in the British people, something that had lain dormant for so long. And not just in white people."

Fired by his own ideology he stared passionately into her eyes. "There are so many people like that, Sadie — people who love their country but are afraid to show it. The French love France, the Americans love America, yet for some reason, when it comes to the British, we're labeled racists. I blame the Left; they've been peddling the same Imperialist self-loathing for so long the entire population believes it. Not anymore. Judging by the traffic on our website the country is slowly waking up."

Sadie couldn't get over how much Michael had changed; his absolute confidence. "Sounds like you're on a mission."

"You could say that."

"Listening to you speak tonight you certainly won me over. And I don't give shit about politics." She sipped her drink. "Dad reckons it won't be long before you become an MP. He's even put a bet on it. And he's never wrong when it comes to things like that. It's why he's made so much money."

"Well I can't thank him enough for his generous donations. It's allowed us to compete with the big parties when it comes to media coverage. I must admit, I didn't recognise him when I saw him tonight. I only twigged when I saw you sitting next to him. You haven't changed a bit."

"*You* have!" She moved closer. "I'm intrigued."

VIII

Michael entered the Cabinet Room with his director of communications Madeleine Stewart, a forty-three-year-old flame-haired Scot from Edinburgh. A former press officer for the Scottish Conservatives, she had moved to London a decade earlier to become the *Daily Telegraph's* senior political correspondent. Because of her deathly-white complexion and ruthless ambition, Madeleine was known around the press corps as Lady Macbeth. She had been the first journalist to champion Michael after hearing him speak at a GB Patriots rally in Birmingham. Dazzled by his charisma and the straightforward way he had of putting his message across — a message laced with patriotic fervor — she realised she was witnessing something unique, something she never thought possible; a flag-waving, multi-ethnic right-wing gathering.

It took her breath away to see black and Asian people cheering Michael to the rafters as he condemned in the strongest possible terms the madness of uncontrolled immigration, woke sentimentality and the watering down of British values. A series of up-beat articles followed, charting his meteoric rise from unknown defence lawyer to one of the country's 'politicians to watch', in which she labelled him a 'renaissance man'; a label that stuck.

Appearances on *Newsnight* cemented her position as the 'go-to' journalist on all things Michael Taylor, as the BBC attempted to wrap its corporate, multicultural-head around this strange political phenomenon, asking questions such as "How is it that a working-class black boy brought up during the Thatcher years in a deprived area of Manchester, whose own parents struggled to get by, how is it possible for him to hold such right-wing views?"

Madeleine shook her head in frustration, asking the interviewer, in her penetrating Edinburgh brogue, "Why does the BBC constantly keep referring to him as the 'black' leader of a right-wing party? Or the former 'black' defence lawyer'? You're defining him by the colour of his skin, as though implying he's somehow different, as though he's unable to think for himself. That's extremely condescendsing if you don't mind me saying, and something I thought you were dead against. After all, you've been banging on for years about how equal we all are, while at the same time — and this is what's confusing — you draw attention to people's ethnicity: British Asian, Black British, Afro-Caribbean. So which is it? And also, it seems by your line of questioning that Michael doesn't exactly fit into your idea of what a 'black' person should be. Surely he can be whoever he likes? After all, we don't live in North Korea...

"Michael is all about collectivism, not splitting people into groups the way the BBC like to do.

Michael has never made an issue of his race. In fact, as far I can see, race has got nothing to do with what GB Patriots stands for. The only criteria for joining the party is, are you patriotic? That's it. Not, where were you born, what your religion is or what skin colour you are? Just that; do you love this country? So what you *should* be asking is; what are Michael Taylor's views? What does he believe in?"

Madeleine took a sip of water and stared at the interviewer. "Forgive me, but your surname, its Bengali isn't it?"

"What's that got to do with it?"

"Exactly."

"B… but surely he's anti-Muslim!?" said the presenter, getting irate. "It says so in his literature!"

"Alright. Calm down. Dear me… Let me clear this up right now. Michael is not anti-Muslim. He's anti-Islamist, There is a difference. In fact Muslims are free to join the party. Many have, as a matter of fact. Michael is against anyone who wants us to change our society by forcing their religion and culture down our throats, expecting us to adapt to their rules, then bombing our citizens if we don't acquiesce. After all, Britain is a Christian country, and he wants to keep that way."

Delighted with the interview, Michael emailed the next day to thank her. A close professional relationship began, culminating in Madeleine being offered a job in his administration, the other members of which were on their way to Downing

Street for the first cabinet meeting since GB Patriots came to power.

An overwhelming sense of power washed over Michael as he entered this historic room. The symbol of collective government since the eighteenth century, he gazed in awe at the famous boat-shaped cabinet table around which momentous events in the life of the nation had taken place, not least Churchill's iconic speech marking the end of the Second World War. For some reason Margaret Thatcher came to mind — the antichrist according to his father — sitting in the prime minister's chair ruling her cabinet with an iron fist.

He was desperate to sit in that chair, but felt self-conscious with Madeleine in the room. Glancing at the portrait of Sir Robert Walpole above the fireplace he said, casually, "If you don't mind I'd like to collect my thoughts before everyone arrives."

"Of course Prime..." She quickly corrected herself at his insistence. "Sorry. Michael," and left the room.

The chair was already pulled aside, as if an invisible hand was inviting him to sit. He walked over and sat down, sinking into the padded red leather. Placing his hands on the table he felt a river of history flowing across its polished surface. He thought about his ancestor Bartholomew Francome Taylor. Michael visualized him walking up the gangplank of the *RMS Trevelyan* in 1838, free from the sugarcane estate owned by Lord Francome that had held him captive since birth; free from the shackles and the branding iron, the letter 'F' not only burnt into his skin but, like all slaves on the Francome estate, into the very fabric of his name — setting out on a journey that would eventually lead to this room. To this very chair. Never in his wildest dreams would he have thought such a thing was possible...

1838? Who was sitting here in 1838? Michael ransacked his prodigious memory… *Let's see... that would be… William Lamb, Viscount Melbourne. The most powerful man in the land yet he couldn't stop his wife having an affair with Lord Byron. There's a lesson for you.*

Michael looked at the empty chairs surrounding the cabinet table; soon they would be filled with his handpicked team; some of the brightest, most talented patriots in the land; a multi-ethnic group drawn from all levels of society, although Michael was keen to stress it was their talent and love of country that got them the job, not their race or gender. Two of the most senior posts — Chancellor of the Exchequer and Home Secretary — had been allotted to the grandchildren of immigrants. David Yip's family had emigrated from Hong Kong in 1901, settling in Liverpool's Chinatown district, the oldest in Europe. By the time David was born the Yip's owned a string of Cantonese restaurants and Oriental food wholesalers throughout northwest England. He was educated at the prestigious Blue Coat School then went on to study economics at Cambridge, gaining an honours degree. Head-hunted by Goldman Sachs he spent four years in New York before returning to London. Michael first met him in the bar of the Adelphi Hotel in Liverpool following a GB Patriot's rally. After introducing himself they fell into a discussion about the dire state of Britain's finances and the inability of successive governments to kick-start the economy post-Covid. What impressed Michael, apart from his fervent patriotism, was his daring solution to the country's woes, namely a massive investment program funded by government to completely modernise Britain's creaking infrastructure, wiping away all vestiges of its Victorian past. Instead of a sporadic injection of a few hundred billion pounds here and there, like former administrations, David proposed spending trillions on road, rail, housing and the NHS, making Britain the envy of the world, all of which would be recouped when the economy burst into life. Although they were the same age, Michael was struck by David's youthful appearance, his grasp of economic matters and his visionary ideas. He immediately invited him to join his inner circle, calculating that, if by some miracle his fledgling party ever came to power, David Yip would make the perfect Chancellor, an appointment guaranteed to make the powers that be in Beijing sit up and take notice.

Michael's choice of Home Secretary was equally daring. Grace Magars was a forty-one-year-old former Border-Force inspector of Nepalese ancestry. She was descended from a prominent Gurkha family from Central Nepal who had served in the British Army since the regiment's inception over two hundred years ago. Her great-grandfather, Kulbir, had come to live in Britain in 1919 after serving with distinction in World War One. Although most Gurkha troops were sent back to Nepal at the end of the conflict, Kulbir was given special dispensation to remain after he fell in love and married a Welsh nurse who had tended his injuries in a field hospital close to the front line.

Grace grew up in Brighton where her fiercely patriotic views were ridiculed by her trendy school friends, who labelled her old-fashioned and out of touch. Following a brief period working for Army intelligence she was head-hunted by the UK Border-Force who offered her the post of Inspector. Disillusioned at the lack of proper funding, the low morale of the staff, the ineffectual powers she had at her disposal, she became a whistleblower, her devastating critique published in the *Mail on Sunday*. The article was brought to Michael's attention by Sadie's father, David, who suggested contacting Grace and inviting her to the next GB Patriots rally. Grace accepted, meeting up with Michael soon after.

An explosion of flashbulbs lit up the Cabinet Room. Frenzied shouts were heard from the media pack gathered across the street. "Mr. Yip! Mr. Yip! Which cabinet post are you expecting?"

Michael looked up to see the youthful figure of David Yip breeze pass the window on his way to the front door.

IX

Emma and Michael's new home was a detached, double-fronted Victorian property located on Hall Road, a short stroll from Wilmslow town centre. With good-sized bedrooms, three receptions rooms, dining room and study, it was large enough to accommodate their two children when they visited on weekends. Richard and Haley had recently flown the nest; Richard studying chemical engineering at St. Andrews University, Haley — the artist of the family — attending Goldsmith's College of Art in London.

Despite only moving in a month ago Emma had worked wonders with the dreary interior, her creative skills transforming the gloomy place into bright, well-lit rooms furnished with cream sofas and sash curtains that puddled satisfyingly onto thick shag pile carpets. The style was modern genteel, although the kitchen was a high-tech gleam of polished chrome and marble. Even though the house had a large cellar, Michael insisted on installing a smoked-glass air-conditioned cabinet to house his growing collection of vintage wine; a legacy of his visit to the Hudson mansion over two decades ago. Sadie's influence ran deep.

Thankfully things had calmed down on the Rodwell front; it seemed Khan was keeping a low profile. And Michael knew why; he'd been popping over to Levenshulme a couple of times a week on his way back from Manchester, making sure to park right outside the front door. Khan had obviously been tipped off that the defenseless old man wasn't so defenseless after all; that he had a family who cared about him; a wealthy family, judging by the top-of-the-range BMW.

Michael took a sip of Châteauneuf-du-Pape before cutting into his beef Wellington.

"So how's the first month been? Settling in?"

Emma gave an ironic chuckle, "It's a lot busier than Burford. I've never worked in such a large practice; twelve GPs! But everyone seems to get on OK. My patients are nice enough. You get the odd awkward one, like most practices, but yes, everything's fine." She flashed one of her cheeky smiles. "I'm just glad I don't have to deal with Lady Goddard anymore. Oh my God, talk about a pain in the backside! She treated me like her own personal physician!"

"She spoke to me a week before we moved you know."

"*No!* You didn't tell me."

"I thought I'd spare you. I was just coming out of the bank when she ran up to me and said, in that plumy voice of hers, '"I've just heard that your wife has decided to move up north. It's not on you know!"'

Emma cringed. "No way! What did you say?"

"I told her I was sorry but we don't live in feudal

times anymore so you were free to do as you like."

"You *didn't!?*"

"I did."

"*Michael!!*

"You should have seen her face. She turned round and flounced off down the High Street."

"I *bet* she did! Oh Michael that's so funny." She took a sip of wine. "I was thinking, why don't you invite Rodwell over this weekend? He's not seen the house. We could take him into town for a meal? Or you could cook?"

"Great idea. I can show him those new retirement apartments while he's here."

"Any sign of him wavering?"

Michael sighed. "Not really. You know how stubborn he is. Although when I saw him two nights ago he was complaining about the damp in his bathroom."

"That's dangerous for someone his age."

"Tell me about it. I didn't say anything though."

"Why not?"

"Because he'd think I was trying to pressure him into moving. It has to be his decision. If I can just get him to look at those apartments, he'll see how nice there are and hopefully come to his senses."

"Hopefully." Emma glanced through into the lounge and saw a news report on the TV showing migrants crossing the Channel in an inflatable dingy. "Those poor people."

Michael looked the screen and shook his head.

"It's ridiculous. Why don't they claim asylum in the first safe country they land in? Why do they have travel all the way to Britain? Because we're a soft touch, that's why. Always have been."

"You're not saying they risk their lives just to claim benefits?"

"If it looks like and dog and barks like a dog…"

"They're fleeing war."

"War's got nothing to do with it. Most of them are from peaceful countries like Albania and Pakistan. They're economic migrants, pure and simple."

"A lot aren't."

"OK then. Let's say this country was at war with Scotland, and Wales was a safe haven. Why would I travel all the way to Sicily? Because that's what they've done, only in reverse."

"They've probably got family over here."

"We can't just travel to wherever we want. There are laws. And if you break the law you're a criminal, not matter what nationality you are. We should be like Australia, and have a points system."

"But they're desperate. They just want a better life."

"So do half the population of Africa. Not to mention the whole of North Korea; all twenty-five million of them. Should we let them in?"

"Of course not. They should be assessed on a case by case basis."

"That's what *I* want; a system that's fair to both the migrants *and* to the people of this country, who, let's not forget, are footing the bill for all this largesse. That's what these left-wing luvvies don't realise; the money has to come from somewhere. So yes, I agree, migrants should go through the proper channels, like they had to do years ago. What they *shouldn't* do is cross over illegally. I'm telling you, if the government doesn't get a grip they'll be anarchy. The NHS can't cope as it is. Look at all the people from Hong King who've arrived recently. They all need dentists and GPs. But at least they came here legally. And you won't find them moaning about their rights and trying to change the country with their stupid religion. If it was up to me I'd let more of them in."

"You're all heart Michael."

He reached across the table and took Emma's hand. "You know your problem, Em'. You're too soft."

Emma smiled, "I must be, marrying you."

"Look at the state of this lot."

The next day Michael was in the main office of ITS Legal speaking to one of the junior barristers about a case he was working on — the trial of a man accused of murdering his boss — when the head of chambers, Peter Rosen, called him to the window. He walked over and stood beside him. The window overlooked St. Anne's Square. A small group of far-right protestors waving Union Jacks were gathered beneath the statue of Richard Cobden.

Peter shook his head. "Bloody fascists."

Michael stared at the fluttering flags and anti-Islamic, anti-immigration placards. A bald, tough-looking man in his forties wearing a denim jacket and jeans started howling through a mega-phone, but because of the double glazing they were unable to hear.

"Typical thug!" said Peter. "Not one brain cell to call his own... My grandfather fled the Nazis you know. He'd turn in his grave if he saw this lot."

At lunchtime, as Michael was crossing St. Anne's Square, he came across a flier on the ground left by the far-right protesters. He picked it up, tucked it into his pocket and headed to his favourite Italian restaurant.

Waiting for his starter to arrive he took out the flier.

'WAKE UP BRITAIN! OUR COUNTRY IS BEING STOLEN!'

"Would you like a drink, sir?"

Startled, Michael rammed the flier into his lap. "Oh!.. Yes!.. I'll erm… I'll have a small glass of Barolo please. Sorry about that. Miles away."

"That's OK, sir. I'll get your drink now."

"Thank you."

He glanced around the room to make sure no one was looking then glanced again at the flier. Beneath the headline was a photograph of a dinghy packed with migrants crossing the English Channel. On the reverse was the logo of 'GB Patriots' — the head of a snarling pit bull. Below was a short article which began 'Every day, hundreds of rapists, pedophiles and drug-dealers enter this country illegally. And what is our so-called government doing about it? NOTHING! These vile scum…'

Shocked, Michael screwed it up and shoved it into his pocket. Later, as he made his way back to his chambers, he threw it in the bin.

Rodwell and Emma walked into the kitchen arm-in-arm. Michael, wearing a chef's apron, was poised over the cooker.

"Well, Granddad. How do you like the house? Not bad is it?"

"Not bad? It's wonderful! And so *warm*. Every room! You wouldn't think it was snowing outside."

"That apartment I told you about is like that — wall-to-wall central heating."

Rodwell's smile vanished. Emma glanced at Michael, shaking her head.

"Yes," continued Michael, quickly changing the subject. "We don't usually get snow in November. Hope it stays around for Christmas. Not long now. You're coming over this year aren't you, Granddad? Richard and Haley will be here."

Rodwell's smile returned. "If you'll have me?"

Emma gave him a hug. """Of course we'll have you! Now, what can I get you to drink? Beer or wine.?

"Oh, wine please. Red if you've got it. My GP reckons it's good for my heart."

Emma opened the state-of-the-art smoked glass

cabinet. "Always listen to your GP."

"Open that bottle of Margaux," said Michael, about to drop three fillet steaks into the frying pan.

Emma gave a mock gasp. "Oh, Rodwell! You're *very* honoured. Michael was saving that for a special occasion!"

"This *is* a special occasion! How do you like your steak, Granddad — medium, well done?"

"Well done, please. I can't stand blood on the plate."

"You're just like Michael," laughed Emma. "He likes his burnt to a crisp."

"Don't listen to her."

"Your father liked his steak well done," said Rodwell."Not that he had it all that often."

Now it was Michaels's turn to look gloomy. Emma noticed. She took Rodwell's arm. "Come and sit down. It'll be ready in a minute." She led him to the dining table, sat him down and lit the candles. "I hope you're hungry?"

"Starving!"

"That's what we want to hear," said Michael, taking the dauphinoise potatoes out of the oven. "I've cooked us a feast."

While Emma went to open the wine Rodwell took in the spacious kitchen and beautifully laid table. He thought about his usual Friday night back at Victoria Street — fish and chips in front of the gas fire, no one to talk to but the television. He could have this every week if he took them up on their generous offer… No. He just couldn't bring himself to sell the house; too many memories.

Emma handed him a glass of wine. "Penny for thoughts?"

"Oh I was just thinking… Ooh! Nice wine that… I was just thinking how fast Christmas comes around. Time flies these days."

"I know what you mean. It was only yesterday I was changing Haley's nappy. Now here she is, getting ready for her end-of-term show."

"Always was artistic that one. I remember her sending me a beautifully drawn card for my eightieth. She must have been what, seven, eight?"

"Five."

"Five. Well there you go. Always was talented."

Michael began plating up. "I don't know where she gets it from. I was useless at art at school."

"So was I," agreed Emma.

"And how's Richard doing? Michael said he's getting married next year. Bit young, isn't he?"

"Old head on young shoulders; like his father. He couldn't be more opposite to Haley, who's turning into a proper rebel. You wouldn't think they were twins."

"Right! Food's ready!" cried Michael, expertly carrying all three dinner plates over to the table.

Rodwell was amazed. "Where did you learn to do that?"

"In a posh restaurant in central London."

"*You* were a *waiter?!* Never!"

"It's true! I worked there for three months while I was at Middle Temple. I know all the tricks; how to serve wine properly," he winked, "how to charm the customers into leaving a big tip."

"Now that I *can* believe!" laughed Rodwell. "Charm the birds from the trees that one."

Emma smiled. "Tell me about it."

After dinner Emma served coffee in the lounge. A lover of true-crime books, Rodwell asked Michael about his latest case.

"Oh! This one's a peach," he said, putting a couple logs on the fire.

"I know. I read about it in the paper... I mean, fancy murdering your own boss; shooting him as he was getting out of his car. Evil sod. According the *Evening News* he hasn't got a leg to stand on."

Michael laughed. "It's a good job you're not on the jury Granddad. I'd be scuppered."

"Why? You don't think he's innocent, do you?"

"It doesn't matter what I think. My job is to defend him. I will say this though, things aren't what they seem."

"Go on."

"I can't say anymore, sorry."

"Don't leave me in the dark!"

"Sorry Granddad. I'd lose my job if I told you. You'll have to wait until the trial to find out."

"When does it start?"

"First week of February."

"Can you get me on the jury?"

"You'd be no good. You've already made your mind up!"

The next day Michael and Emma took Rodwell into Wilmslow for lunch. As they were strolling back to the house Michael gave Emma the pre-arranged signal; it would sound better coming from her.

She took Rodwell's arm. "Would you like a quick peek at that retirement apartment we told you about? It's just along this road? I'd love you to see it."

Emma had been so nice to him he felt he couldn't refuse. "Oh go on then. Just a quick look."

So far so good. "And it's only a two minute walk from our place," added Michael.

The Beeches was a small, three storey development with a live-in warden set in landscaped gardens. Straight away Rodwell liked the security gates — no chance of anyone putting dog shit through the letter box.

"The apartment's on the ground floor," said Emma. "According to the brochure it looks out over the back garden."

Michael pointed to the sign on the gate — 'Show Apartment Open' — and said, in mock surprise. "Look at that! Talk about good timing."

The perfect partner-in-crime, Emma went in for the kill. "Do you fancy having a look?"

Rodwell knew what they were up to. Nevertheless

he played along. "Might as well, seeing as I'm here."

Michael pressed the buzzer on the gate post and explained they wanted to look at the show apartment. A few seconds later the gates swung open and they made their way inside. They were greeted by the agent, who showed them around. Rodwell couldn't believe how nice the apartment was. The open-plan living room was luxuriously furnished, with a kitchen-cum-dining area to the right which led on to the main bedroom and small guest bedroom. To the left, French windows opened onto a spacious patio. The bathroom had a walk-in bath and shower and was covered in gleaming white tiles. Everything about the place smelt fresh and clean. Rodwell's mind was in a spin. To think he only had to say yes and the apartment would be his. He tried to hide his enthusiasm, but Michael could tell he loved it.

On the drive back to Levenshulme Michael purposely avoided any mention of the apartment. Turning into Victoria Street the contrast was all too obvious. Pulling up outside number 22 he glanced at his granddad; the look on his face said it all.

Around 10.15 p.m. that night Michael's mobile rang. It was Rodwell. "Thanks for having me over. Really enjoyed myself... I…I can't get that apartment out of my mind. It was absolutely gorgeous."

Michael nudged Emma who was sitting next to him on the sofa. Emma sat up and leaned close to the phone.

"Can I ask you something, Michael? How much

is it?"

"Don't worry about that. It's a gift from Emma and—"

"Just tell me."

Michael had prepared for this moment. "Two hundred thousand," he lied, halving the true price. "Absolute bargain for Wilmslow."

"I'm very tempted… That's not a yes. Let's just say I'm considering it."

Michael ended the call, high-fiving Emma.

X

"FOR AS MUCH AS IT HATH pleased Almighty God of his great mercy to take unto himself the soul of our dear brother Rodwell here departed: we therefore commit his body to the ground; earth to earth, ashes to ashes, dust to dust; in sure and certain hope of the Resurrection to eternal life, through our Lord Jesus Christ. Amen."

"Amen."

Michael stared at the coffin. He felt numb, unable to comprehend what had happened. Just as his grandfather was on the brink of selling his house and moving into the retirement apartment fate had cruelly snatched him away. But fate had nothing to do with it. Despite what the death certificate said — 'heart attack' — Michael knew it was murder. Cold-blooded murder. And he knew who was behind it — Shoaib Khan. Not through physical violence of any sort, but by months and months of intimidation. Drip by poisonous drip. Of course he couldn't prove it; as a lawyer he knew full well hearsay doesn't stand up in court. But Khan was behind it alright. Every fibre of his being told him so.

He had thought about sharing his suspicions with the police, but quickly dismissed the idea; he knew how badly stretched they were. Understaffed, underfunded, with rock-bottom morale, they barely had the resources to prosecute open-and-shut cases, let alone one as complex as he grandfather's. Justice, it seemed, was a thing of the past.

A light dusting of snow began to fall as Michael, Emma, Haley and Richard slowly left the graveside. They were the only mourners, apart from a nice man from The Korean War Veterans Association who laid a wreath of poppies. Although numerous cards and flowers had been sent by Rodwell's neighbours, including Aleena and Haniya, Michael was adamant that no Muslims would attend the funeral. He took one final look at the grave, windswept in the bitter January cold, then he led his grieving family back to the car park.

Christmas had begun so well, Richard and Haley arriving two days before to help Emma decorate the house: an old family tradition. On Christmas Eve, after Michael phoned Rodwell to say he'd pick him up at 10 a.m. the following morning, they all went into Alderley Edge for a meal.

Haley was a bundle of energy in the discreet surrounds of the French restaurant, telling everyone the latest goings-on at Goldsmiths. Michael couldn't get over how like Emma she was in both looks and personality. With her light, coffee-coloured skin, blue eyes, full lips and frizzy, apple-blond hair, she was often mistaken for a Brazilian. Richard on the other hand was a degree darker, inheriting Michael's hazel-coloured eyes and prominent cheek bones. His personality too was like his father's; studious, sharp as a razor, with a keen, adventurous spirit.

At last Richard managed to get a word in. "I've taken up golf, Dad."

"Oh my God!" laughed Haley. "You'll be voting Tory next!"

"Nothing wrong with that," said Michael.

"All the students play," continued Richard, steering the debate away from politics — the last thing he wanted was for Haley to start spouting her left-wing views. "It's hard not to when you go to St. Andrews. You'll love this, Dad. They have this ancient tradition that gives students right-of-way on the course."

"Really?"

"Goes back to sixteen something or other."

Still Haley couldn't resist. "The only reason you chose St. Andrews was because Prince William went there."

"Of course he didn't," said Emma, coming to her son's defence. "It's one of the best universities in the country."

But Richard could look after himself. "The reason I went to St. Andrews Haley is because it's miles away from Goldsmiths!"

Michael laughed. *"Touché!"*

"Anyway," said Haley, calling a truce; it was Christmas Eve after all. "I hope you're all coming to my spring show. It's been inspired by the recent..." *Migrant crossings,* thought Michael, second-guessing his militant daughter, "—Frida Kahlo show I went to see at the Pompidou Centre last month. Mind blowing! Ahead of her time that woman."

Michael was on time on Christmas Day, pulling up outside Rodwell's at 10 a.m. sharp. He got out of his car and glanced up and down the street; apart from his grandfather's not one house had Christmas decorations up. *Typical! They live in this country but they won't follow our traditions! I mean, how hard can it be? When in Rome and all that.*

He knocked at the door. Silence. He knocked again. He waited, thinking Rodwell might still be in bed. He bent down and shouted through the letterbox, "Merry Christmas Granddad! It's me: Michael! Chop, chop!"

He waited and waited. Not a sound. Something was wrong. He could feel it. *Shit!* He hurried to the end of the street, turned left and cut down the back alley, a route he'd taken many times as a child when he wanted to surprise his grandfather. When he arrived he found the back gate was locked, so he climbed onto a wheelie bin and jumped over the wall. Rodwell always kept a spare key to the back door under one of the plant pots. Michael lifted a couple up until he found it. Trembling, he put the key in the lock and let himself into the kitchen. The house was silent.

"Granddad?... Granddad?"

He noticed the table had been laid for breakfast — cereal bowl, side-plate, teacup stamped with the crest of The Royal Northumberland Fusiliers, his old regiment — something Rodwell did religiously every night before going to bed. It was now ten past ten. Why hadn't they been used?

He pushed open the kitchen door. "Gran—" Rodwell was lying in his pajamas slumped against the front door. "GRANDDAD!" Michael dashed down the hall and crouched over him. "Oh Granddad! What's happened?" He lifted his wrist, desperately feeling for a pulse. He was stone-cold to the touch. He'd obviously been dead for hours. Michael let out a howl. *"NO!!!"* Sobbing, he cradled his lifeless body in his arms. *"Granddad! Granddad!"* Instantly he visualized what had happened — sometime in the early hours there was a BANG! BANG! BANG! BANG! on the front door. Rodwell — stressed, in a daze — must have got out of bed and made his way down the stairs. BANG! BANG! BANG! BANG! BANG! "Who is it? What do you want?" BANG! BANG! BANG! BANG! Confused and frightened, his heart racing, he staggered towards the front door. "Bugger off you bast—". That's when his heart must have given way and he collapsed against the door, dying alone in the freezing hallway. Oh yes, it was murder alright.

After the funeral Michael was in no fit state to drive, so Emma took the wheel. Cruising down the M56 his mind was in turmoil; six months his grandfather had suffered, six long months of stress and anxiety. And what was *he* doing while all this was going on? Living the life of Riley in the Cotswolds. *I should have done more. I should have done more!* His logical side kicked in. *Stop it!* He could torture himself till Kingdom Come but it still wouldn't alter the fact that Khan was the cause of all this misery. So shouldn't he pay him back for what he'd done? He knew how to get to him. No problem.

The day after he visited Rodwell back in October Michael had hired a private investigator to delve into Khan's background — where he lived, where his children went to school, his shadowy business practices. In the end Michael knew more about him than his own wife. Born in Lahore, Pakistan, in 1972, he'd been in and out of prison before coming to the UK in his twenties. Despite having a criminal record he was allowed to settle and start a new life. This 'new life', according to the private investigator, consisted of associating with members of an Asian drug gang who operated in the Cheetham Hill area of Manchester. While most of the gang where either sent to prison or fled abroad, Khan was never convicted. Mr. Teflon then went into the used-car business before gravitating into property, making a fortune buying rundown terraced houses and renting them out to students and fellow immigrants from the Indian Subcontinent. Twenty years of being a Slum Landlord had paid handsomely; he now lived in a detached mansion in the affluent suburb of Hale Barns, drove a black Bentley Convertible and sent his children to private school.

When the private investigator showed Michael a magazine article about him, anger turned to blind rage. There was Khan, dressed in a dinner jacket, smiling as he accepted the award for Asian Businessman of the Year at a swanky dinner at Manchester Town Hall. *Who says crime doesn't pay?* Michael's thirst for justice was so strong that for a brief moment he actually thought about putting a contract out on his life — he knew enough shady characters from his years as criminal defence barrister — but quickly came to his senses. Mulling over the terrible affair he knew that bringing down one shady businessman wouldn't make the slightest bit of difference in the greater scheme of things; Khan was just another example of Britain's lax, open-door policy when it came to immigration. The whole rotten system needed tearing down and rebuilding. But which political party had the guts to do it? Certainly none of the mainstream.

XI

Michael glanced at his hand-picked team of ministers gathered around the cabinet table, each one leaning forward enthusiastically, eager to get on with the job. As well as his Chancellor and Home Secretary — David Yip and Grace Magars, who were sitting either side of him — he was surrounded by a core of hard-line patriots, all of whom had won massive majorities in their respective seats at the recent general election. The one thing they had in common, apart from Michael, was that none of them had ever served in government. Not even a brief stint on their local councils. In fact, lack of experience was essential when being chosen to represent GB Patriots at the ballot box. Michael had insisted on this long before the election, and it turned out to be major vote-winner. He gauged correctly that the British pubic were sick and tired of professional politicians who made promises they knowingly couldn't keep while things got gradually worse — the rich getting richer, public services falling apart, the proliferation of food banks, thousands of illegal migrants flooding into the country unchecked.

The assassination of King Charles proved what he'd been saying all along; that instead of everyone pulling together during a time of crisis, the country was so fractured with ethnic diversity it would tear itself apart. And that's exactly what happened, triggering a general election.

Michael finished laying out the key aims of his administration and waited for the hammering on the table to die down. The first minister to comment was Major Jess Evans — his new Defence Minister — a tough, uncompromising Welshwoman in her early forties. Born in the Rhonda Valley, she had joined the army straight from school, served with distinction in Afghanistan before going on to train young army cadets at the Royal Military Academy, Sandhurst. Inheriting a love of the military from her late father, a former soldier in the Welsh Guards who had fought in the Falklands War, she was a straight-talker

"I couldn't agree more, Prime Minister. If we're going to deliver for the British people it's time we started funding our armed services properly. They're in a woeful state. Russia could walk in tomorrow and there's very little we could do, especially now the United States have pulled out of NATO," She glanced at David Yip. "I just hope the Chancellor agrees with me."

David nodded. "Absolutely. They will get all the money they need. As it states in our manifesto, I will triple the amount spent by the last government. And that goes for public services — education, transport, the NHS... As for pensions and social security, from now on they will only be available to British people. What this says to everyone around the world is,

Britain is no longer a soft touch."

More hammering on the table.

Michael opened the file in front of him and pulled out the GB Patriots glossy election manifesto, proudly holding it aloft. "Speaking of which. I promise everyone in this room, as I have to the British people, that everything set out in this document will be delivered. No ifs, no buts. We will not only rebuild our country, we will rebuild the very fabric of our society, village by village, town by town, city by city, purging it of negative elements. We will banish self-doubt, instill in our citizens a sense of national pride, long since undermined by the Left. We will create an environment where people can come together instead of sticking to their own ethnic communities, striving for the common good. The common good of *everyone!* And we will do it by completely dismantling the education system so that our children are no longer taught a fractious and distorted view of their own history. After all, it's the next generation that will enjoy the fruits of what we're starting here."

Michael looked at the eager faces surrounding him, the electric stares and pumped-up body language. "But first and foremost we will deal with the most urgent of all issues — the creeping Islamification of Great Britain. And we will start right now." He slammed his fist down onto the table, shaking the glasses and carafes of water. "ARE YOU WILL ME?!"

Across the road from the Cabinet Office a Sky

News reporter was doing a piece to camera when suddenly a huge cheer erupted inside Number 10.

XII

It was almost midnight when Michael sent the last email of the day to his junior defence barrister; tomorrow was the start of the murder trial, and he wanted everything in place before walking into court.

Michael switched off the computer and stretched out in his red leather office chair, yawning. He sat for a moment enjoying the calm of his study. The house was silent, Emma having gone to bed hours ago. Two weeks had passed since his grandfather's funeral. Even though the trial consumed his every waking moment, the memory of what happened to Rodwell continued to gnaw at him; the injustice of it all. And every time he switched on the TV there they were, boatloads of illegal migrants wrapped in blankets being led ashore by the Dover coastguard. Watching as they boarded a fleet of coaches bound for God knows where, he wondered how many were potential Shoaib Khans? To Michael the whole thing was symptomatic of country that had lost its soul, a country ruled by a Liberal Metropolitan elite who cared more for the rights of migrants than they did for the British people. What was it again; the famous quotation enshrined in law? — 'The first duty of government is to protect its citizens.' Well, that had obviously been forgotten, along with protecting the country's borders. Not that he blamed the migrants;

they only wanted a better life. No, he blamed the politicians and Whitehall bureaucrats for allowing it to happen. Hearing their mealy-mouth excuses on TV every night after enraged him.

The country was crying out for leadership; someone with strong patriotic values, someone who could stand up to the politically-correct fascists of the Left.

OUR COUNTRY IS BEING STOLEN!

Michael blinked. *Whoa! Where did that come from?*

Then he remembered the leaflet he'd picked up in St. Anne's Square. He was dog-tired and wanted to go bed but something made him restart his computer and type 'GB Patriots' in the search box. As the website uploaded his heart began to race.

Straight away he could tell by the homepage that GB Patriots were a bunch of politically naïve thugs — bright garish colours, overtly racist slogans, repellent images of migrants huddled round a campfire captioned with the words 'FILTH!' and 'SCUM'. Nevertheless, like a seasoned prospector panning for gold, he could see a faint glitter amongst the swirling pebbles and stones.

He clicked on the contact page and saw a familiar face — the tough-looking bald guy he'd seen from his office window that day bawling into a megaphone. His name was Steve Farrell, leader of the fledgling party. Farrell was thirty-eight-years-old and described himself as a 'pissed-off patriot.' Below was a 'GET IN TOUCH' box. Careful to use an encrypted email, Michael typed this short message…

Hi Steve. I saw your protest in St. Anne's Square a few weeks ago. I agree with what you say, but not how you say it. If GB Patriots are serious about gaining political traction then you must soften your image and become more palatable to the British public. Image, after all, is everything… A well-wisher.

Michael's finger hovered over the keyboard; he knew if he took this step there was no going back. He held his breath and pressed 'send.' Suddenly the void inside him — the emptiness he felt so keenly that evening in Sainsbury's car park listening to 'Holding Back the Years' — began to fill, drop by intoxicating drop.

The first few weeks of the trial were plagued with delays, mostly from the prosecution insisting on new evidence being submitted, much to the annoyance of the judge, which pleased Michael no end. Even more pleasing was the fact that the jury — warned beforehand the trial would be a lengthy one — were constantly asked to vacate the courtroom while legal technicalities were discussed. Knowing how important it was to have the jury on his side, Michael would subtly shake his head and raise his eyes, leaving the jury in no doubt that he too was annoyed with the antics of the prosecution.

At the start of week four Michael had a meeting with Peter Rosen, head of chambers, to discuss the case. When he returned to his desk he wrote an email to his defence team outlining the strategy for that day. He was just about to leave for court when an email popped into his 'in-box' marked GB Patriots.

Hi well-wisher. Thanks for your email. I formed the party three years ago. We're only small, around a hundred members. So yeah, we need all the advice we can get. What's the score? Are you interested in joining? Be happy to meet up for a chat. Or you give me a call via the contact number on the website. Rule Britannia. Steve.

"Michael."

Michael closed his laptop as Peter Rosen approached his desk. "Yes, Peter."

"Judith and I are having a dinner party on Saturday; nothing formal, just a few friends. Would you and Emma like to come?"

"Err.. yes. Look forward to it."

"Great... Good luck today."

When the court broke for lunch Michael took his laptop to a nearby Starbucks and reread the email. *Three years ago and only a hundred members. No wonder!*

He thought carefully before typing his reply.

Hi Steve. I'd love to meet but I'm afraid I'm rather busy at the moment. In the meantime, if you want to attract more members you need to change your website. The garish colours and racist language are off-putting. British people don't like being hectored. We're a moderate lot. As I said in my email, most people agree with what you say, so tone things down and make the website more professional. Take a look at the Conservative and Labour websites. I know they've ruined this country, but sometimes you can learn from your enemies. Also, your logo needs to change. A Pit Bull? Seriously! May I suggest the humble acorn. An acorn signifies renewal, optimism, hope for the future. That's what this country needs right now. Remember, mighty oaks from small acorns grow. Be in touch. And as you so righty say, Rule Britannia.

"All this nationalism sweeping Europe right now," said Peter Rosen, cradling his glass of red wine. "It's very worrying."

Everyone nodded. There were ten people sitting around the candle-lit dining table in Peter's Alderley Edge mansion — various wealthy couples he'd known for years.

"I know what you mean," said Irving Tellerman, a successful jeweler from Hale. "Look at Italy, and their right-wing prime minister."

His wife Mona, a sociology professor at Manchester University, agreed. "Sweden's heading the same way by the looks of things, so is Greece."

Determined to remain impassive Michael had been silent throughout the whole conversation. Nevertheless he found himself saying, "Cause and effect though, don't you think?"

Emma flashed him a worrying look.

"Cause and effect? In what way?" asked Mona.

"Uncontrolled migration; if the government won't do anything about it that's when people turn to extremist parties. Take Sweden; you couldn't get a more liberal-minded lot. So for them to start electing right-wing politicians then something is seriously wrong with the system."

Peter saw that Mona was about to about to jump down Michael's throat. He rose quickly from the table. "Dessert anyone?"

In the car going home Emma hardly spoke. Michael knew why. He took her hand.

"Sorry, Em'. I couldn't help myself. That woman. How she can say—"

"It's not just tonight Michael. You've been acting strange for some time."

"Strange?"

"Distant. Not yourself. You're obsessed with migrants all of a sudden. It's all you ever talk about. There's nothing you can do about it so why get stressed?"

"I don't want our grandchildren growing up in a divided country, Em' that's all. Our culture's being watered down."

"You sound like an extremist."

"An extremist!? What's extreme about wanting a proper immigration policy?"

"Please don't shout, Michael."

"Typical bloody snowflake."

"Put yourself up for election then, if you feel *that* strongly about it."

"I might just do that."

Exasperated, she let go of his hand. "Oh… do what you want. You always have done!"

"What's that supposed to mean?"

When they got home Emma went straight upstairs to bed. Michael poured himself a whiskey and sat in his study, brooding. He switched his computer on. There was an email from Steve Farrell marked 'new website'. He clicked on the link. He was amazed. The website had undergone a complete transformation — gone was the snarling Pit Bull logo, replaced by a golden acorn attached to a cluster of oak leaves.

Like it! Very 'ancient Rome'.

In place of the harsh colours and racist propaganda the Homepage was now a serene and friendly information hub with a header of rolling images — green fields, well-kept market towns, idyllic country villages populated by smiling white faces. Michael was thrilled; he couldn't have designed it better himself. OK the actual wording left a lot to be desired, and the lack of racial diversity was a problem. But it was a big improvement on the blaring rhetoric he encountered last time. He clicked on 'contact page' and found the number. He glanced at the clock — 11:06pm. *It's a bit late... Sod it.*

He grabbed his mobile off the desk. Switching his phone to 'hide caller ID' he dialed the number.

A wary Mancunian voice answered. "Hello?"

"Is that Steve? Steve Farrell?"

"Who's this?"

"Well-wisher."

It took him a moment before the penny dropped. "Ah! The mystery man! Right."

"I've just been on your website. Or should I say your *new* website... Congratulations. It looks amazing."

The voice suddenly relaxed and gained warmth. "Cheers. Yeah. One of our members works in IT. I told her what you said and she redesigned it. Seems to be working; it's only been live for less than a week and we've got ten new members. Like you said, image is everything. So err… thanks for the advice."

"Pleasure. Just one thing; the information on there — what you stand for, your political aims — still sounds rather amateurish." He thought about mentioning the lack of racial diversity but decided to leave that for another time.

Rome wasn't built in a day.

"If I were you I'd get someone to rewrite it."

"How about you? You seem to know what you're talking about. Better still, why don't we meet up? Let me buy you a pint as a thank you… Hello?"

Caught off guard, his heart racing, he answered before he could think about it. "Sure, why not."

"Great stuff. Are you free tomorrow?"

He suddenly lost his nerve. "Can't tomorrow I'm afraid. Family commitments."

"How about next week? Monday lunchtime in the Sawyer's Arms on Deansgate?"

"Yeah, yeah. OK."

SHIT!!!!

"Perfect. I'll email you to confirm… I'd ring, but I notice you've hidden your number. What's with the cloak and dagger?" He laughed. "You're not a member of the security services are you?"

Michael kept it jovial. "Like James Bond you

mean? No, I can honestly say I'm not a secret agent."

"Wouldn't matter if you were. We're not doing anything illegal."

"You were previously, which is why I suggested toning-down your message."

"I see… What's your name by the way? *That's* not a secret is it?"

"Of course not… It's Mike."

"See you on Tuesday then Mike."

Michael's voice took on a cautious tone. "I erm… I need to tell you something before we meet… I'm bl—"

"Hang on. You're not a tranny are you?"

Michael stifled a laugh. "No… Look, forget it. See you on Monday."

XIII

At lunchtime Michael left ITS legal and walked across St. Anne's Square towards the Sawyer's Arms on nearby Deansgate. He was both nervous and excited — like his first day as lead defence barrister at Oxford Crown Court in the trail of Arthur Smith, an elderly sub-postmaster from Witney accused of murdering Ariditi Sokoli, a twenty-two-year-old Albanian migrant. Woken in the dead of night by a masked Sokoli brandishing a kitchen knife, Smith was dragged downstairs and ordered to open the safe. Terrified, fearing for his life, his fingers scrambled round the dial. But the combination eluded him. Pleading for more time Sokoli kicked him in the face, punching him with a knuckleduster as he lay on the ground. About to blackout, Smith grabbed a screwdriver from the bottom shelf of the counter him and plunged it into Sokoli's eye, killing him instantly. Despite being offered a manslaughter plea by the prosecution, Michael wanted the case thrown out on the grounds of self-defence, appalled that Smith might have to serve time in prison for merely defending himself and his family. During the trail the prosecution painted Sokoli as a hard-working family man who had come to the UK in the hope of a finding better life. Smith, on the other hand, was accused of being an old-fashioned bigot. They even dug up a witness who testified they'd heard Smith uttering anti-immigrant comments in the post office on the day of the break-in. The jury found Smith guilty of murder, sentencing him to twelve years in prison. After the verdict was announced it was revealed to the jury that Sokoli was far from being the law-abiding citizen made out by the prosecution; he was in fact a violent criminal who had committed several offences whilst in the UK and had managed to avoid deportation after the intervention of an immigration lawyer who successfully argued it would be against Sokoli's human rights as he was married to a British woman who was pregnant with his third child.

It was Michael's first case, and he'd lost it, an experience made worse by the sarcastic jibes aimed at him by the prosecution team as he left court. Walking down St. Giles on the way back to his chambers he seethed at the injustice of it all.

The Sawyers Arms was on the corner of Deansgate and Bridge Street. A well-known Manchester landmark, it had served drinkers since 1771. It was one the pubs Michael's father used to frequent on a Saturday night when he was a teenager; a meeting place for him and his mates before they headed off to one of the city's nightclubs.

About to cross the busy road Michael stopped for a second, staring at the pub's distinctive red, yellow and cream glazed tiled frontage. He pictured the door opening and a young Joel stepping out, laughing and joking with his friends.

He crossed the busy road and pushed open the door. He was met with the warm smell of booze and the hum of lunchtime chatter. In the corner, to his left, a TV placed high on the wall was showing horseracing, the sound muted. Mindful of who he was about to meet he made his way to the bar and ordered a pint of bitter. Taking a sip he casually turned and surveyed the room over the rim of his glass; it was crowded with the usual city-centre clientele — office workers, shoppers, construction workers in high-viz vests — but no Steve Farrell. Michael felt strangely relieved. He took another sip. Suddenly there he was, emerging from the Gents and making his way back to his table beneath the TV. He was wearing a dark-blue denim jacket, black trousers and off-white trainers. Michael leaned against the bar and took a moment to size him up; medium height, thick-set, he looked as though he could handle himself; his shaven head and four-day stubble accentuating his tough persona. Every time the door opened and someone walked in Farrell stared at them nervously, trying to figure out if it was 'Well-Wisher'. The fact he was equally as nervous calmed Michael somewhat. He was about to walk over but stopped; despite being one of the best defence barristers in the UK, famous for his scrupulous preparation and concise opening remarks, it was only now he thought to himself...

What the hell do I say?... Sod it.

He picked up his pint and made his way across the room. Steve Farrell glanced up for a second at the handsome black man as he approached, his eyes locked on the entrance door. Michael put his pint on the table.

"Sorry, mate, I'm expecting someone."

"Hi, Steve… it's me: Well-Wisher."

Farrell froze. He recongnised the voice but… He turned his head slowly and stared open-mouthed at the smiling, confident black man dressed in an immaculately tailored suit towering above him. Although Michael had rehearsed this moment countless times, he had no idea what Farrell's reaction would be — shock (obviously) aggression, violence even? What he didn't expect was cringing humiliation, like he'd just been made a fool of. Farrell turned puce. Breathing rapidly he snatched up his bottle Becks and gulped half of it down, his eyes scanning the table in front of him.

"Is this a joke?"

Buoyed by his reaction, Michael said, calmly, "No joke... I'm a patriot, just like you."

Still no eye contact. "Bollocks, you're black."

"What's that got to do with it?"

Desperately trying to formulate some sort of answer as to why, being black, Michael couldn't be a patriot, Farrell's brain went into overload. There was a split second when the mist began to clear, but then just as quickly clouded over. He shook his head.

"Narr."

Michael pulled back the chair and went to sit down. "You and I are no different, we both want the same —"

Farrell jumped to his feet. "I'm out of here."

"Steve. Listen—"

"Fuck you."

Michael watched as he pushed his way through the crowded pub and disappeared out of the door. He picked up his drink and sighed. *What was I thinking?*

"I don't know why I bother to cook," said Emma, glaring at him from across the dining table. "All you do is sit there brooding. Talk to me for God's sake!"

Irritated, his mind replaying the disastrous day he'd just had, he fired back, "Fine! What do you want to talk about!?"

"Anything! How was your day?"

He recalled the testimony of a prosecution witness who had demolished a major part of his client's defence, the disastrous meeting with Farrell, and then later, back at his chambers, his disagreement with Peter Rosen over the strategy of the case.

"Shit, if you must know."

"Well that's not my fault! So *don't* take it out on me!"

"I'm not taking it out on you! You asked me and I told you!"

Silence.

"Aren't you going to ask about *my* day?"

Michael stabbed at his mushroom risotto. "How was your day?"

"Like you're interested."

He shot up from his chair. "I can't win with you, can I?!" He stormed out of the kitchen, grabbed his jacket, opened the front door and left.

It was a balmy May evening so he headed for The Carrs, a nearby beauty spot where locals walked their dogs. He was desperate for some fresh air; somewhere quiet where he could think. Walking beside the River Bollin his mind was in turmoil. It wasn't just the crappy day he'd had that depressed him; it went much deeper. Things hadn't been right with Emma since Rodwell's funeral; a fracture had developed in their relationship, a fracture that kept on widening. Not that he blamed his wife. There was only one person to blame for all this: the person who'd caused all the heartache in the first place — Shoaib Khan.

Just then his phone pinged. It was an email from Steve Farrell. Michael sat on a bench and opened it.

Had a good laugh today did you? Pathetic. Do yourself a favour and crawl under the rock you slithered out from.

Oh! Someone else wasn't happy with him! *Form a queue why don't you!* Fuming, he called Farrell's number.

"Hello?"

Michael let rip. "You ignorant bastard! I take time out my busy day to meet you and you have the nerve to walk out without even listening to what I had to say! *I'm* the one who advised you to change your pathetic website, don't forget, and that's how you treat me! I really don't know why I bothered—"

"Whoa! Whoa! Whoa!!" Amazingly Farrell was

still on the line! "Who the *fuck* d'you think you're talking to?"

"Who d'you think *you're* talking to?!"

"A fucking time-waster!"

"You're the time-waster!"

"Me?! In case you hadn't noticed pal, you're black!"

"And?"

"What d'you mean 'and?' We're right-wing patriots, for fuck's sake!"

Cool as you like Michael said, "So am I? In fact, I'm probably more patriotic than you."

"Bollocks!"

"It's far from bollocks, I can assure you."

"What, stopping immigration and sorting the Muslims out? Are you for that?"

"Absolutely."

"Turn the small boats round in the Channel? Smash the Left?"

"The sooner the better."

"Balls!

"That's all you've got to say is it, 'Balls'? Not, 'Oh, how interesting; a black guy wants the same things I do. Please tell me more.'"

Farrell's voice lost its aggressive edge. "Hang on. Are you for real?"

"If you'd have stayed in the pub instead of walking out you wouldn't be asking that question."

There was a moment's silence as Farrell took this in. He burst out laughing. "Fuck me! I don't believe this!"

Michael's voice remained serious. "Why not? There are lots of people like me; people who, because of their colour or where they were born, aren't considered patriotic. It couldn't be further from the truth. In fact, there's a massive group of us out there just waiting for the right party to come along… Now the question is, Steve, is that party GB Patriots?"

"Hang on. You're not suggesting we—?"

"That's exactly what I'm suggesting."

"Never in a million years."

"Before you dismiss the idea, ask yourself this; are you content to be just another right-wing fringe party, moaning from the sidelines about the way things are and not getting anywhere? Or are you serious about getting into power and changing this country? And by that I mean for *everyone.* If you are, then I think we should meet… Think it over and let me know."

Michael ended the call, his revenge for this afternoon's snub. He turned to walk home when suddenly his mobile buzzed — an email from Farrell! Expecting a volley abuse, he opened it.

OK you made your point. Let's meet.

"I can't believe I'm doing this," said Farrell, nervously tearing open a sachet of sugar and tipping it into his coffee.

"Neither can I," countered Michael.

It was the next day and they were sitting in the

hushed surroundings of the Royal Exchange Theatre Café'. Above their heads, frozen in time, was the old trading board, a poignant reminder of the buildings original function as a stock exchange. The theatre itself lay silent behind smoked glass. But the real drama was taking place on table four, although to an outsider it was just two friends having a quiet chat.

Farrell took a sip of coffee. "I've been thinking about what you said…"

"And?"

"I want you to know that I'm not a racist."

"Of course you're not, Steve," laughed Michael. "Some of your best friends are black."

Farrell jumped to his feet. "Fuck you."

Michael grabbed his arm. "Sorry, Steve… Please… Please… I'm listening. "

Farrell sat down, exhaling loudly. He gathered his thoughts. "This country's being taken for a ride. Hundreds are sneaking in daily, thousands for all we know, and the government are doing fuck all about it. I wouldn't care if they were blonde, blue-eyed Swedes. The fact is, they're coming here illegally. Worse, they're being allowed in unchecked, from cultures that hate what this country stands for. You'd think they'd be grateful, wouldn't you? But oh no. I mean, look at that Libyan bastard who bombed the Manchester Arena. We took his father in, educated his sons, housed them, fed them, free of charge, and look how they repaid us — by killing and maiming innocent teenagers. And again, what does our government do? Fuck all.

"'Oh, he was just a one-off', they say. So what if he was? One's too many as far as I'm concerned! I mean, how would *they* like it if one of their children had been killed? He wouldn't be a one-off then, would he! But what they can't seem to get into their thick, privileged skulls, is that if we hadn't let his father in in the first place, it would never have happened. 'But he was fleeing oppression', scream the Left. So fucking what! There's oppression all over the world. What are we supposed to do? Let everyone in? According to the Left we should. And it's not just the UK. It's the same across Europe… I mean, have you *been* to Paris recently? Fuck me, the streets are filled with half of Africa and the Middle East. There's robberies, rapes, you name it. Now I ask you, why should anyone put up with that, just because some liberal politicians tell them to? Who, by the way, live in gated houses in the posh parts of town and have houses in the country to escape to every weekend, leaving ordinary Parisians to deal with the shit. And don't get me started on the Muslims, who hate our guts and want to change this country with their warped religion!"

Michael noticed Farrell was shaking. He was moments away from losing it.

"I couldn't agree more, Steve. So let's do something about it?"

"Like what? No one listens."

"That's because you're not reaching the right people."

"And who are the 'right people', exactly?"

"The ordinary British people… Of *all* races: people who think the same as you but are too scared to say it." Now it was Michael's turn to get worked up. "I'm taking about hard-working, patriotic people of Asian, Chinese and Afro-Caribbean descent who love this country, whose ancestors fought and died for it. Do you *really* think they agree with what's going on? Well take it from me, Steve, they don't… It's like we're being forced to take part in some mass experiment."

Steve blinked rapidly for a few seconds, contemplating an idea so far-fetched his mind could barely grasp it. But the seed was planted, and started to grow. He raised his head as though straining to hear a distant sound. "So what you're saying is…"

After years of cross-examining people in the witness box Michael could tell Steve was struggling to find the right words. "What I'm saying is, Steve, there are literally millions of people like me; people who are desperate to show their loyalty to this country. But how? Joining the Conservatives is no good; they just get patronized. Believe me I've been there. Labour's a waste of time; all *they* do is tell them to be proud of their heritage. I mean, what good is it telling an inner-city kid whose grandparents came over from India in the last century, whose only connection to the 'old country' is a trip there once in a blue moon, who has nothing in common with the place and more than likely can't wait to get back to the UK...

what good is it telling them to be proud of their heritage? The UK *is* their heritage. So why not tell them to be proud of that? But oh no; that's racist! As for the Liberal Democrats, forget it... Now, imagine if all these people joined GB Patriots. Imagine how powerful the party could be — black, white, Asian, Chinese, all marching together with one aim in mind; to make this country great. Within months it would be a force to be reckoned with, a wrecking ball that smashes the political establishment. Quite honestly, Steve, if that happened, they wouldn't know what hit them."

Steve Farrell could hardly believe what he was hearing. It was as if a mass of dark clouds had suddenly parted and he could see the summit of a mythical, sunlit mountain. He shook his head, unable to speak. In the end he just looked at Michael and laughed. "Fuck me."

Michael wanted to give him time to think, so he got up from the table. "Another coffee? My shout."

He nodded. "You better put a brandy in it."

When he returned to the table Steve looked pensive.

"A lot of the members won't stand for it, Mike. Goes against what they believe in."

"Kick them out. Simple as that. We don't want people like that in the party."

"'We'? Thinking of joining?"

"Why d'you think I'm here."

"Seriously? You wanna join a right-wing party?

A black guy?"

"Deadly."

"Fuck me sideways. That's absolutely brilliant, Mike.... Hang on. I'm gonna have to speak to the membership first." He imagined doing just that. "They'll think I've lost it."

"Fine. I wouldn't want to join a party that doesn't want me... Oh, and do me a favour Steve, stop referring to me as black. I'm British, like you, and proud of it."

XIV

Two weeks later Michael received an email from Steve Farrell inviting him to speak at the next GB Patriots meeting. He was stunned. Farrell explained that half the membership had resigned in protest, while the rest were 'waiting to be convinced.' This was the moment he'd secretly been craving; a platform to launch his political career. If he could win over a bunch of hardcore right-wingers then anything was possible.

Just as his renewed interest in politics was bearing fruit his relationship with Emma began to sour. These days they barely spoke, and slept in separate rooms. Michael wasn't stupid. He knew if he continued to neglect his marriage it was only a matter of time before it came to an end. But the lure of politics was too strong. Showing the same focus and determination that propelled him towards a stellar career as a defence barrister, he ignored the difficulties and carried on regardless, convinced he was doing the right thing. After all, he said to himself, sacrifices were necessary if he wanted to achieve his goal. What that was at this stage he couldn't say. All he knew was, deep down there was a void that needed to be filled.

The meeting was held in a function room above an old Victorian pub in Sale. Steve met him in the bar with the ominous words, "They're all upstairs waiting for you. Would you like a drink first?"

If Michael was nervous,, he didn't show it. He gave a cocky smile. "That's OK. Let's get this show on the road."

Steve led him out of the bar, down a short corridor and up a flight of threadbare, carpetted stairs. The air was stale, the wallpaper stained and peeling. The pub was built when the British Empire was at its height. Now look at it. Approaching a door at the top of the stairs Michael could hear a hum of conversation coming from inside the room. As soon as he entered it went deathly quiet. A host of white faces stared at him; some were curious, others hostile. All were eager to see this anomaly, this freak of nature. They were sitting in three rows forming a large semi-circle, mostly men of varying ages, although a few women were present, their heads shifting, trying to get a better look.

Steve rubbed his hands together nervously. "Right guys. This is Michael; the bloke I was telling you about. I'm sure you'll be interested to hear what he has to say."

Michael stood in front of them, his immaculate black suit and pressed white shirt in stark contrast to the casual clothes surrounding him. The scene was similar to a courtroom on the first day of a trial, seconds before he put his case to the jury. That's what he was doing now. Despite that, when he opened his mouth to speak nothing came out. He cleared his throat.

I should have had that drink.

Silence. A truck rumbled past shaking the floor, while in the distance a police siren faded.

"Well?" asked an unseen voice.

Michael blinked, unable to speak.

"Get on with it!" shouted a voice at the back.

"Hey! Less of that!" barked Steve. "He didn't have to come here you know!"

Michael saw his opening. "That's right, Steve. I didn't. I could have stayed at home and left you to it — meeting here once a week, angry and frustrated; watching from the sidelines as Britain slides further down the pan; not a snowball's chance in hell of ever changing things. I didn't because, like you, I care deeply about this country." He looked at each person as he spoke, walking slowly from one side of the room to the other. "Does that surprise you; a black person talking like that? Thinking like that? Well, it shouldn't. There are millions more like me out there; proud patriots who are just as frustrated as you are." He stopped in the centre of the semi-circle. "Speaking of patriotism, I noticed on your website that the secretary of the party is an Adam Novotny. Is Adam here tonight by any chance?"

A tall, blonde-haired man in his thirties with Slavic cheekbones wearing a red bomber jacket, jeans and black polo-neck jumper sitting in the front row slowly raised his hand.

"Hi, Adam… Your surname: Novotny… It's Czech, isn't it?"

"Yeah. My grandfather came to this country when the Nazis invaded Czechoslovakia in nineteen-thirty-eight." Adam puffed out his chest. "He was a Hurricane pilot during the Battle of Britain. Finished the war with a string of gallantry medals."

"That's amazing, Adam. You must be proud of him."

"I am. Very."

"Can I ask you something? What type of Hurricane did your grandfather fly? There were twenty-four in total."

"I've no idea."

"That's OK. I'd love to hear more about him later?"

Novotny shrugged, "Fine". He glanced with an amused expression at his friend sitting next to him, an older man called Carl, a tough-looking veteran of far-right rallies.

"Your grandfather came to Britain in nineteen thirty-eight, you say?

"That's right."

"Well, unlike you, *my* great, great, great grandfather arrived a century before, in *eighteen* thirty-eight. Since then my ancestors have fought and died in every major conflict since the Boar War. That's right; *my* family — a *black* family — has served this country faithfully for almost two hundred years... So in effect, Adam, I'm more British than you."

A mixture of shock, anger, and amusement registered on the faces of the audience.

Michael continued. "And that's why I've come to speak to you tonight... You see, it shouldn't matter what the colour of your skin is, or where your family originate. What matters is, do you love this country and everything it stands for? If the answer is yes, and you've come here through the proper channels, and want to add to society and support our values, then as far as I'm concerned your skin colour is irrelevant. Because let's face it, being white doesn't necessarily mean you're patriotic. Quite the opposite, in fact. If you look at the evidence, it's white people who've got us in this mess in the first place."

A wave of nervous laughter went round the room. An unseen voice shouted, "He's right! Look at *The Guardian* and the BBC. Those bastards have been undermining this country for years! Slagging off our history, telling us what we should and shouldn't think, encouraging mass-migration. Our own people! Fucking traitors the lot of 'em!"

A dark-haired women in her fifties stood up. "Shoot the bastards!" A cheer lit up the room.

Michael went on, "I couldn't have put it better myself. But those people are nothing compared to previous governments and the faceless Whitehall bureaucrats who served them; systematically dismantling our borders, allowing thousands of people to flood in unchecked — mostly young men from countries where girls with their heads uncovered and their flesh exposed are seen as fair game — changing the face of this country forever.

Ninety-nine point nine percent of those people are white. So what does that tell you?"

A woman in the second row raised her hand. "That those in charge don't give a shit about ordinary British people!"

"They don't," agreed Michael. "They think more of foreigners than they do of us. Especially Islamists. They're frightened to death of them."

That seem to ignite the room.

"Dead right!" shouted another unseen voice

Michael continued, fired by an inner passion. "Some councils have already changed the name of Christmas so as not to offend Muslim 'sensibilities'. *Some* councils have given in to the Muslim Council of Britain's request to serve Halal food in our schools. Can you imagine going to Pakistan — where Christians are persecuted by the way — and telling *them* to change the name of Ramadan and serve ordinary meat in their schools?! They'd drag you into the street and burn you. But oh no. Not over here. Makes your blood boil!"

The audience was amazed at the sheer charisma of the man standing in front of them, of the amazing things he was saying. They were on the edge of their seats, exchanging grins, shaking their heads in wonder, glancing at Steve Farrell as if to say, 'Hey, you were right about this guy!'

Michael strode up and down the room in full flow, feeding off the febrile atmosphere he had created; gesticulating wildly, pointing accusatory fingers at imaginary foes. "So *my* message to Muslims is, if you *don't* like it, if you *don't* like the way we do things in this country, if it affects your 'sensibilities', then pack your bags and get out!"

Like the rest of the room Steve Farrell had been whipped into a frenzy. He shot out of his chair. "'Cos if you don't, we'll fuckin' well *kick* you out!"

Michael added the spark. "And *I'll* be the one doing the *kicking!*"

The room exploded into raucous cheers. People stood up, clenching their fists and punching the air. Then it happened; a slow, steady chant, started by Steve Farrell and taken up by the rest of the crowd, "Michael… Michael," until it rose to a crescendo that shook the room, "*MICHAEL! MICHAEL! MICHAEL!*"

Building on the success of his initial speech, within a month GB Patriots had elected Michael as their new leader. Steve Farrell gladly stepped aside, becoming his number two. Letting go of the reins so easily surprised Michael; after all, he was the founder of the party.

One night, after a party meeting, he had a quite word with Adam Novotny in the bar downstairs. "Steve knows his limitations," explained Adam. "He's taken us a far as he can. After what happened to his daughter that night he's desperate for change, and realises you're the man to do it."

Michael was confused. "Why? What happened

to his daughter?"

"Didn't he tell you?"

"No."

"She was killed in the Manchester Arena bomb attack."

An inner circle soon coalesced around Michael; a trusted policy-making group consisting of Steve Farrell, Adam Novotny and Jill Chambers. Jill was an unassuming thirty-eight-year-old hospital administrator from Sale in Greater Manchester. With her steel-rimmed glasses, frumpy clothes and mousey demeanor she was the classic wallflower. But behind that quiet façade was a born organiser with exceptional IT skills. It was Jill who had redesigned the GB Patriots website.

The first policy decision to be made was by far the most important — immigration. It was decided that a five-year moratorium would be implemented. During that time a new department would be set up — The Department for Internal Security. Consisting of more than three thousand highly-trained staff, their function would be to clear the backlog of illegal migrants; identifying, processing, then swiftly deporting. After years of half-hearted policies and gross underfunding by previous governments, Michael was determined to create a properly-funded department that would finally solve the problem. Once the backlog was cleared, new immigration rules would come into force; strict vetting procedures whereby only those wishing to contribute to the UK — who respected the laws of the land and had the means to support themselves for ten years without claiming benefits — would be allowed to settle. At the same time a new visa system would come into being that monitored people entering and leaving the country. In order for the system to run smoothly it was decided that a complete overhaul of the Border-Force would need to be carried out. Priority was also given to deporting foreign criminals who were clogging up British prisons.

In the weeks and months that followed, numerous small-scale rallies were held up and down the country. Everywhere Michael spoke he was greeted with the same response — incredulity, followed by downright amazement.

The rallies began to attract more and more people from ethnic minority backgrounds, which shocked many on the Left. Whites too flocked to the meetings, all eager to hear his patriotic message. What pleased Michael most was how well everyone mixed, getting together in the bar afterwards to share their stories. Gone were the usual barriers of race, class or gender that normally kept people apart. Instead, everyone felt equal, united by a single defining aspect — love of country. It was exactly what Michael had envisaged for the party, and he was thrilled. Not everyone was happy; a few party die-hards like Carl refused to accept the situation and left. But with hundreds of new members joining every week, that hardly mattered. But it was far from plain-sailing; Michael received death-threats, and a private security company needed to be hired to protect each of the venues from masked left-wing thugs who threw bottles and shouted insults at those attending.

One night, after a particularly bellicose rally in Birmingham, Michael was approached for an interview by Madeleine Stewart, senior political correspondent for the *Daily Telegraph*. She'd heard a rumor, she said, about a new political movement that was set to break the mould, and had come to see for herself.

"I have to say, Mr. Taylor, I've been inv—"

"Michael, please."

"Thank you. I have to say, Michael, I've been involved in politics since I was at university, but I can honestly say I've never seen anything like tonight. It was a revelation. Really. I'd love to write a piece about you — your background, what drives you."

"Of course."

"How about an interview tomorrow, over lunch?"

"Perfect."

The following afternoon Madeleine caught the 4.30 train to Euston and went straight to the office to write the article. It appeared the next morning on page 4 under the headline, 'A New Dawn in Politics?' where, in breathless prose, Madeleine wrote about her experience attending the GB Patriots rally; her encounter with its charismatic leader, his background and political views.

The media, hungry as ever for novelty, were quick to pick up on the story, and it wasn't long before all the major broadcasters featured this new political sensation, setting in motion a chain of events that would dismantle the age-old political system. Extreme left and right wing parties were outraged; the left calling him a traitor, the right convinced he was a Trojan Horse of some sort. A host of conspiracy theories flooded the internet — Michael was a Russian spy, a CIA operative, an Establishment puppet, an agent of the Chinese Communist Party; one group going so far as to claim he was a Japanese-built AI robot financed by a group of African dictators who wanted revenge for the slave trade. The fact was that nobody, least of all the mainstream political parties, knew what to make of him, unable to grasp he was simply a man with a message.

One man who understood was Sadie's billionaire father David; as a successful hedge fund manager he had the unique ability of spotting trends and predicting outcomes amid a forest of seemingly chaotic data. He knew instinctively what was going on, and how it might benefit him in the future. Keen to remain anonymous at this early stage, he used an intermediary to contact the party secretary Steve Farrell and began making large donations. As the party's membership skyrocketed, huge amounts of money from a diverse range of donors flooded in. People from all walks of life gave generously. When Steve saw the amount of British-born black, Asian and Chinese multi-millionaires who not only joined the party but gave large donations, he knew Michael's message had broken through. The healthy state of the party's finances meant that Michael could give up his job as a barrister and concentrate full time on politics. Which was just as well — Peter Rosen, his boss at ITS Legal — was so outraged after discovering Michael's political views he was already planning to fire him.

As Michael became more and more famous so his personal life spiralled out of control. His wife Emma moved out and filed for divorce; his left-leaning daughter Haley refused to speak to him. The only family member who stood by him was his son Richard; unlike Haley he had no interest in politics. It was this fact above all others that David foresaw in his crystal ball — the fact that Michael appealed to people who were apolitical and naturally distrusted politicians; who made decisions purely on gut instinct. In other words, the vast majority of British people.

XV

"I, George Finch, as acting returning officer for the Tatton constituency, do hereby declare that the number of votes cast for each candidate were as follows... Louise Perry, Liberal Democrats: three thousand and twenty-four. Stuart Henry Grayson, Conservative Party: fifteen thousand one hundred and forty. Alan 'Tear-It-Down' Tyler, Cheshire Anarchists; thirty-one. Shirley Manning, Labour Party; ten thousand six hundred and fourteen. Michael Bartholomew Tay—"

A cheer went up in the hall.

The acting returning office held up his hand. "Please... Please... Thank you... Michael Bartholomew Taylor: GB Patriots; twenty-four thousand nine hundred and seventy-six."

The hall erupted, camera flashes lighting up the stage. A Sky News camera focused in on each of the candidates as, grim-faced, they shook hands with the victor. The only person smiling, apart from Michael, was Alan 'Tear-It-Down' Tyler.

"I hereby declare that Michael Bartholomew Taylor will serve as Member of Parliament for the Tatton constituency."

Heart pounding, Michael glanced into the crowd. Sadie and her father David were among a large group of flag-waving supporters at the foot of the stage. Sadie blew him a kiss. David fist pumped.

Steve Farrell grinned and shook his head as though he was dreaming. A surge of adrenalin coursed through Michael's body as he stepped up to the microphone. He thanked the acting returning officer, the police, and his campaign team. He then produced a piece of paper from his jacket pocket.

"This result marks a seismic shift in the political landscape of the United Kingdom. Beginning here in Cheshire, the present government is on notice that they have lost the confidence of the British people. Voters have made it clear that they want to see an end to traditional party-politics — left against right, rich against poor, black against white — a system that has lost itself in a maze of political correctness and wokesim, a system that has done so much damage to this great nation of ours. Because, as we all know, what's bad for the hive is bad for the bee. And by that principle I promise to serve the people of this constituency."

Another huge cheer went up.

Michael raised his hand. "Finally I would like to read a quote from the former Home Secretary Suella Braverman. At the time she said this it was derided as 'dog-whistle' politics. These are her exact words; words that sent a chill down my spine, words that first started me on this journey." The hall fell silent. He began to read from the paper in his hand. "'We need to wake up to what we are sleep-walking into: a ghettoised society where free expression and British values are diluted, where Sharia law, the Islamist mob and anti-Semites take over communities. We need to overcome the fear of being labeled Islamophobic and speak truthfully. Enough of the hand-wringing and apologies. Turning a blind eye to fanatics has got us into this terrible situation: it needs to stop.'"

Michael lowered the piece of paper and stared directly into the lens of a BBC News camera. "People of Great Britain, it's time to wake up."

The by-election had been triggered by the sudden death of the incumbent Tory MP Elaine McAvoy, who died of a heart attack during an official visit to a children's nursery in Wilmslow. She was Michael's MP and had held the Tatton seat for over a decade. Convinced it was fate, Michael immediately added his name to the ballot paper. He was now well-known in the area, especially in the village of Alderley Edge, where he lived with Sadie following his divorce from Emma. Her penthouse apartment became the nerve-centre of operations, her father's huge wealth financing the six-week election campaign. With countless volunteers drafted in to blanket the area with leaflets and posters, thousands of pounds was spent on radio and newspaper advertising, ensuring GB Patriots had an equal profile with the three major parties. Because of this, and the sheer novelty of his candidacy, Michael was interviewed numerous times on television and radio, allowing his message to filter out across the rest of the UK.

The result sent shockwaves through the country. No one had given Michael a chance: the media, political pundits, the Westminster elite, all of them comparing GB Patriots to the Monster Raving Looney Party. But Michael knew better. He realised that the Tatton constituency — the Tories fourth safest seat — had upset the political applecart once before, when Martin Bell dramatically unseated Neil Hamilton in the 1997 general election. But Michael's victory was even more dramatic; in 1997 people voted against one particular MP, whereas in this election they not only voted against the government, but the whole socio-political system.

Analysis of the turnout proved even more intriguing. Later that night, while a victory party was taking place at GB Patriots campaign headquarters in Knutsford, David and Michael were sitting in a back office pouring over the voting figures.

David pointed at a graph on the computer screen. "The amazing thing is, you've taken votes from all three of the major parties in almost equal amounts. It means your message is resonating with a broad section of the population, not just with people on the right. If this was replicated during a general election, GB Patriots would sweep to power."

Michael was thrilled. "Things are about to change, David. I can feel it."

Suddenly the office door swung open and the noise of the party flooded in. Sadie was standing in the doorway holding a bottle of champagne. "Come on you two. You're missing the party."

The next day Michael was contacted by Aldus Mancini, the *Guardian's* senior political correspondent, requesting an interview. Two days later, when he and Sadie were in London for his swearing-in ceremony in the House of Commons, Michael met him at the Marriot Hotel City Hall, directly opposite the Houses of Parliament.

Aldus was already there when he arrived, sitting on the terrace sipping mineral water. Tall and wiry with collar-length black hair, he was casually dressed in chinos, dark-green corduroy jacket, white shirt and red tie. He reminded Michael of his old Geography teacher.

Aldus got up and offered his hand. "Michael. Aldus. Great to meet you. Thanks for agreeing to the interview by the way. What can I get you; tea, coffee?"

"Tea please. White; no sugar."

Aldus gave the order to the waiter and they both sat down. He glanced across the river just as Big Ben struck 11 o'clock."Looking forward to working in the bear pit?"

"Certainly am."

"I've been reading about you for some time in Madeleine's Stewart's column in the *Telegraph.* To be honest I didn't think you stood a cat in hell's chance of winning the election."

"Why's that?"

"Hold on a second." He delved into his pocket and brought out a Dictaphone. Setting it on the table he switched it on. "It's not every day a black guy representing an extreme right-wing party becomes an MP."

"What's the colour of my skin got to do with it?"

Aldus tapped the table nervously. "Are you serious?"

"Very... Please, enlighten me."

"Well, isn't it obvious? Right-wing parties are racist. They hate black people."

"Then why did GB Patriots vote for me as their leader?"

"That's what I'm here to find out."

"Then you're asking the wrong person. You should ask them. All I did was join the party."

"Nevertheless, you can see why I'm asking? This goes way beyond a black person with Conservative leanings."

"A 'black' person with Conservative leanings,' rather than a 'person' with Conservative leanings?"

"You know what I mean."

"No I don't. Like to pigeon-hole people in terms of race, do you?"

Aldus ignored the question. "What I'm trying to get at is, what made you join such an extremist party?"

"I joined because I believe in the same things they do — love of country, a desire to protect our culture, something the mainstream parties have long since forgotten, along with protecting our borders. If that's extreme, then I must be an extremist."

"But surely your culture is Black culture."

"I beg your pardon?"

"Black culture."

"And what is Black culture, exactly?"

"It's…"

"Go on." Michael leaned forward, smirking.

I bet your politically-correct brain is going into overdrive so as not to offend me.

"Well it's…"

"Yes? Go on Aldus, you can do it."

"It's hip hop, reggae, R&B."

Michael leaned back in his chair and burst out laughing. "That's the sum total of black people in your eyes is it: hip hop, reggae and R&B? Why not add drug-dealer and pimp while you're at it?"

"Now you're being offensive."

"*I'm* being offensive!!? *Really!?* You're too funny Aldus."

Aldus squirmed in his chair. "Of course there's more to being black than that. It's about knowing where you come from, and being proud of your heritage."

Michael nodded thoughtfully."'Knowing where you come from.' I see… But I come from Great Britain, and I'm very proud of my heritage."

"What about your father and grandfather?"

"They were born here too."

"Further back then."

"*Further* back!? What, to the Rift Valley? If that's the case then you and I are probably related."

He stared at him and grinned. "Hey! I thought I recognised you. Yo! Aldus, baby! How ya doin', cuz?" Michael took a sip of his tea. "Let's move on before you make a complete fool of yourself."

But Aldus wouldn't move on. Or maybe he couldn't, so ingrained was his political beliefs. "What about all the racism in the 60s where black people were forced to rent substandard accommodation and had to take menial jobs? Doesn't that bother you?"

"Of course it bothers me. But what's the point in harping on about the past? I'm interested in the here and now, and how I can improve things. I admit, there's still a lot of work to done as far as racism and integration is concerned. That's 'work', Aldus, not 'woke'. There is a difference. Hopefully my election to Parliament will help."

"But the past is important. I read that one of your ancestors was a slave. How does that make you feel?"

"Extremely sad."

"Aren't you angry with this country for enslaving him? Don't you think the British State is morally bound to pay reparations, or at the very least apologise?"

"This country's done some terrible things — participating in the slave trade, the Opium Wars — but expecting the present generation to feel guilty about it is ridiculous. As for the government apologising or paying reparations... Let me ask you something. I read that your grandfather came over from Italy in the 1950s. Is that right?"

"What of it?"

"Did you know thousands of Britons were taken as slaves by the Roman Empire; worked to death in some far-off mine or forced into household servitude? Some ended up in the Coliseum, where they were slaughtered for sport. Now, as someone of Italian heritage, do you feel guilty about that? And should we demand an apology from the Italian government? Or ask for reparations? I think not. The fact is, there isn't a country on earth that hasn't done unspeakable things. If we want to build a better world we need to concentrate on the future, otherwise we'll be on a constant merry-go-round of blame and counter blame. And who benefits from that, eh? Nobody. Except perhaps the racists."

Michael did his utmost to steer the conversation towards concrete political matters, matters that affect everyone in society, whatever their skin colour, emphasising again and again his credentials as a none-racially-specific politician. But Aldus seemed incapable of understanding. As Michael joked to Sadie over dinner later that evening, "He was like one of those androids you see in sci-fi films, unable to think outside its parameters."

Sadie laughed. "I know what you mean. My ex-husband had a lot of friends like that; you know, left-wing Parisian intellectuals educated beyond their intelligence. They used to sit around all evening discussing the evils of white society, yet they all lived in beautiful apartments in the whitest parts of town and ate at the finest restaurants. You should have heard the bullshit they came out with. It was pure self-loathing."

Towards the end of the interview Michael realised that if he wanted to get his message across he had to put it in a way that Aldus and his readership would understand. And so, for the first time ever he brought up the subject of his colour, ending the interview with, "What you're witnessing, Aldus, is the evolution of Black consciousness."

A window in Aldus' mind opened briefly as he tried to get his head around such a revolutionary concept. "Yeah, yeah. Interesting."

"Hopefully the day will come when the word 'Black' won't need to be mentioned at all."

But then just as quickly it closed, and once again Aldus stared at him blankly.

Michael sighed. "I don't know, maybe I'm being too optimistic, but that's what I'm hoping for."

When the article came out the following day Michael was vilified not only by the left and the right but by certain Black civil rights groups, who labeled him an 'Uncle Tom'. The long-winded piece was full of insults, accusing him of 'muddled thinking' and 'political naiveté,' someone who had 'turned his back on his proud ancestry', a 'Judas of the worst kind' who 'day after day betrays the cause of black people'. Reading it over breakfast Michael could only shake his head.

Poor guy. He hasn't got a clue.

But what this legendary interview did achieve, as he hoped it would, was spark a debate about what it means to be British in the 21st century.

XVI

WITH NO PARTY LEADER to welcome him to Parliament and show him the ropes, Michael was given a tour of the Palace of Westminster by an official after the swearing-in ceremony. He was then taken down a labyrinth of corridors and shown to his office; a pokey, windowless room containing a filing cabinet, an empty bookcase, and two badly scuffed Formica desks, each with its own desktop computer and telephone. Lord knows when the office was last used; years ago judging by the dried-out carcass of a Yucca plant perched forlornly on top of the filing cabinet.

"That's for your Parliamentary assistant," said the official, pointing at one of the desks.

"Oh yes."

He delved into his pocket and handed Michael a small booklet. "This is given to all new members of Parliament: it's a sort of guidebook pointing out the dos and don'ts… It's very important you read it. There's lots of interesting information in there."

"Thank you."

"Good luck… Oh, and be sure to fill out your expenses form correctly." The official gave a thin-lipped smile and left the room. Michael looked about him and sighed.

Ah well. A journey of a thousand miles…

From day-one he was treated with suspicion by

his fellow MPs, who either ignored him or made derogatory remarks when passing him on the corridor. The only friendly faces were a couple of Conservative backbenchers on the right of the party. But they were quickly told to desist by the Tory Chief Whip. It was like his first day at Grammar school all over again.

His maiden speech came during a debate on immigration, where he ridiculed the government's attempts to stop the ever-increasing number of small boats crossing the Channel. "How come," he said, "we stopped the Spanish Armada, Napoleon and Hitler, yet day after day we're being defeated by a gang of people-smugglers? You ought to be ashamed of yourselves!"

"It's the law, you idiot!" howled one of the members on the government benches.

Michael shouted back, "Well change the law! You're the government, aren't you?!"

During Michael's first year as an MP his profile throughout the country rose dramatically. People from all backgrounds eagerly tuned in whenever he appeared on TV or made a speech in the House of Commons. As the UK economy slid further into recession and sporadic riots broke out in the inner cities, he began to acquire cult status, especially among the younger generation who saw him as a new breed of politician, someone fearless enough to stand up against the Establishment and tell it like it is. His appeal was such that he united all age groups, races and social classes, — from the retired Colonel in the shires to the black kid living in a high-rise council flat — fostering a fervent brand of patriotism unseen in modern times.

Out of all the media appearances he made that year his most talked-about moment came during a debate on BBC's *Question Time.* In the wake of a recent earthquake in northwest Pakistan the panel was discussing the thorny issue of overseas aid.

Shami Akbar, a Labour MP, derided the government's "paltry contribution of twenty million pounds."

Following whoops and cheers from certain members of the audience, Fiona Bruce then asked Michael for his opinion.

He leaned back in his chair and said, laconically, "Let me ask you something, Mr. Akbar. You're a religious man, are you not?"

"Yes. I am a proud Muslim."

"Very commendable. In that case, I'm sure you've heard of the Biblical quote 'Charity begins at home'."

"Of course."

"Well then, I'd like to ask you one simple question if I may. If your son or daughter was having difficulty paying their mortgage and were about to be thrown out onto the street, would you come to their aid by paying their arrears, or would you give that money to the Pakistan Earthquake Appeal?"

Shami Akbar shifted awkwardly in his seat. "That's got nothing to do with it!"

"It's got everything to do with it. Why should the British taxpayer send money overseas when our economy is in recession and people are suffering hardship; especially to a country that spent over five billion dollars on its defence budget last year?"

"We're talking about a humanitarian disaster here, not someone's mortgage! Britain is a rich country, and can easily afford to give more."

"Oh I see," said Michael sarcastically "You think we should give more, do you? " He gestured towards the audience. "Well, I'm sorry if twenty million pounds of these good people's hard-earned money isn't enough for you. But Britain already spends billions of pounds on overseas aid as it is. We're one of the most generous countries in the world. Too generous if you ask me. In my opinion that money could be better spent on our inner cities, where services have been cut and people are having to rely on food banks. And if you're so concerned about humanitarian causes, why is it we didn't hear a peep out of you last year when a tsunami hit the coast of Thailand, killing thousands of people? Is it because those people weren't Muslims?"

"That's outrageous. You're nothing but right-wing, racist scum!"

The audience gasped.

Fiona Bruce interjected, "May I remind you, Mr. Akbar, that this is a civilized debate, and that personal insults are not permitted."

Michael smiled. "That's alright Fiona. I've been called far worse." He then addressed the audience. "Did you notice it didn't take Mr. Akbar long before he played the race card? And *this* from a person who's not only a member of the Muslim Council of Britain, but an active supporter of several Pakistani charities and has business interests over there. Seems to me he's more concerned about Pakistan than he is for his own constituents, who, in case he hasn't noticed, are in the middle of a cost-of-living crisis right now and need all the help they can get. If that's the case, why doesn't he do us all a favour and bugger off there."

Then something amazing happened; GB Patriots started to win seats on local councils. First it was a trickle, then, after the party took control of Cheshire East Council, it turned into a flood. Voters up and down the country saw what a difference a GB Patriots-run council had made to the area, where priority was given to local people in terms of housing, education and social care. Despite the government insisting the council take its share of newly-arrived migrants — whose numbers had soared dramatically over the summer — housing them, providing financial support, including employing costly translators as well as gender realignment therapists, the council dug its heels in and refused to budge, preferring to spend the money on sheltered accommodation for the area's homeless.

The left-wing press were up in arms, labeling Cheshire East 'Britain's first fascist council.' The government, pressured by the liberal media, was forced into action, threatening to take the council to court if it didn't obey the ruling. Then, when it realised that going down the legal route would only give Michael a platform to expound his populist views (already they sensed the political tide was turning) they cut funding from central government.

This was the moment Michael had been waiting for. Over the next two months he wrote numerous articles in the press and did the rounds of all the television stations, castigating the government for threatening its own people by depriving them of basic services; services they themselves had paid for through the tax system, calling them traitors for putting the needs of illegal migrants first. As the rubbish piled up in the streets and the council was forced to close a host of special-needs programs, Michael made a series of short films that were broadcast on all the major news channels, highlighting the worsening situation in his constituency. In one heart-rending film he visited a council-run old-folk's home that was about to close due to lack of funding. He interviewed staff as well as residents, who were close to tears. Standing in the communal lounge the matron pointed to a frail ninety-eight-year-old man slumped in his chair. "That man is a Normandy veteran. He fought for this country, and now he's being thrown out onto the street. Why is the government doing this?" In another, he visited a couple whose severely disabled daughter had been denied access to specialist care.

"It's broken us," said the father.

As soon as the films were aired, TV networks from all over the globe descended on Cheshire. Michael held a press conference in Cottons Hotel outside Knutsford. So many reporters wanted to attend that a large marquee had to be set up outside. To the delight of Russia Today, Chinese State Media and the North Korean News Agency, Michael set out his case, accusing the government of turning Cheshire East into something resembling the Third World, which was exactly the kind of place the migrants had fled from in the first place.

A raised hand came from an American NBC news channel reporter. "You mentioned immigration just then, which is a hot topic in the US right now. I've looked at the figures; most care workers in the UK are from overseas. In fact, the government issued 87,600 visas last year. Can you tell us what your strategy is to deal with this short-fall?"

"Absolutely! GB Patriots will fund social care properly, so that care workers are able to earn the kind of wage that makes this emotionally demanding, physically strenuous job attractive. We will create career pathways for people so that social care is seen as a profession. Not only would it vastly improve the way vulnerable people are cared for, while saving councils from going bust as a result of rising social care bills, but eventually the government wouldn't have to issue thousands of care work visas a year to plug the gaps. And when—"

Suddenly a worried-looking Steve Farrell dashed onto the stage and whispered something to Michael. Horrified, Michael shook his head sadly. "I've just been informed that an elderly lady has died this morning after the ambulance called to take her to hospital couldn't reach her house because the road was blocked with refuse bags." Barely able to hide his anger, he let rip. "The Prime Minister has blood on his hands. He needs to take a long hard look at himself and his misplaced loyalty.... Ladies and gentlemen, before I end the press conference and investigate the matter further, I want to appeal to all fair-minded, patriotic citizens around the world. Our government doesn't give a damn about the British people. They are doing their level best to bully us into submission. So please, I beg you, send whatever help you can."

The council's martyrdom was complete.

Within a week millions of pounds flooded in from charities all over the world. A host of countries, including Japan, India, Canada, the United States, France, Russia and China gave generously. Even poverty-stricken nations like Somali, Mozambique and Malawi gave what they could. But the most embarrassing contribution as far as the British Government was concerned was a two million pound donation from North Korea, sent on the express orders of Kim Jong-un, who appeared on

North Korean television highlighting the plight of "Cheshire East's brave and patriotic citizens. Proof, if proof were needed, of the stupefying folly of the decadent, liberal West."

Two days later the government quietly restored its funding to the council.

Keen to profit from the global publicity, celebrations were held all across East Cheshire, culminating in a huge bonfire on Knutsford Heath, where, on a stage decked-out with Union flags, Michael gave a speech, likening the victory to the glorious defeat of the Spanish Amada, which drove the liberal media apoplectic, as he knew it would.

*

"I've just been told by the chef that dinner will be served in ten minutes. Would you care for another drink?"

Michael, Sadie and David were sitting on the terrace of *Palazzo Giallo*, Angelo Scarpi's magnificent Renaissance villa on the banks of Lake Como. The former hunting lodge of Ludovico Sforza — Duke of Milan and patron of Leonardo da Vinci — Angelo bought the property ten years ago after his telecommunications empire had been successfully floated on the Italian stock exchange. A self-made man of humble origins, he bought it, he told friends, on a whim.

"I'm OK thank you, Angelo," said Michael,

looking out across the lake, its moonlit surface shimmering in the twilight.

"I'll have another!" said David, handing his glass to the white-coated butler. "Just a top-up."

"*Certo.*"

Sadie emptied her glass and did the same.

"*Grazia millie* for coming to see me, Michele," said Angelo, in his strong Milanese accent. "It's been very interesting chatting with you these past few days."

"Likewise. And in such beautiful surroundings."

The so called 'Meeting of Minds' — as Angelo referred to it in the Italian press —had been arranged by David, who'd had business dealings with the Italian billionaire in the past. As the new leader of Lega, a right-wing organization campaigning for strict border controls and a curb on immigration, Angelo saw the opportunity of building an alliance, especially with someone as politically astute and successful as Michael. He wasn't the only far-right leader in Europe to feel that way. Within days of his famous press conference at Cottons Hotel, the leader of France's right-wing populist party the National Rally called to ask if Michael was interested in meeting her. Other invitations soon followed — from Alternative for Germany, Holland's Party of Freedom, Spain's Vox party, Portugal's Chega party and Belgium's Vlamms Belang. What these former colonial countries had in common, Michael realised, was that they too had longstanding, disgruntled black communities firmly settled since the days of empire. Not one of these parties had given them a second thought until Michael came along with his revolutionary message of inclusion. Naturally they wanted to broaden their appeal and increase their membership. All were eager to be photographed with Michael, pick his brains and bask in his recent success.

And so, during the Parliamentary summer recess, Michael, accompanied by Sadie and David, set off on a short tour of Europe to meet these like-minded leaders in the hope of fostering cross-cultural and political relationships; a kind of far-right supergroup, each coordinating with the other to build a strong, Christian-centric alliance that would usher in a political Renaissance.

The last country he visited was Italy, where a cheering crowd of Lega supporters showered him with flowers at Malpensa Airport. From there he, Sadie and David boarded a helicopter and were flown to Lake Como, touching down in the grounds of *Palazzo Giallo* — so-called because of its bright, mustard-coloured walls.

They were met by the butler and led up a sweeping stone staircase into the cool semi-darkness of the entrance hall. After a brief pause to admire the view of the lake through the colossal front doors, they were shown into the *Sala di Mars.* Beneath a frescoed ceiling depicting the military victories of Ludovico Sforza, Angelo and his wife Claretta — a glamorous former TV presenter twenty years his junior — were waiting to greet them.

Short and stocky with dyed, slicked-back receding hair, Angelo wore a baggy linen suit and polished brown brogues with slightly raised heels. He was every bit as charming as his reputation suggested. Nothing was too much trouble for this self-styled 'Man of Action.'

While Claretta took Sadie and David into Milan to enjoy the city's cultural treasures, Angelo accompanied Michael on long walks in the grounds of the palazzo to discuss their Anglo-European alliance.

"This idea of inclusivity isn't a new thing," said Michael, as they strolled along the shore of the lake. "The Romans did it. So did the Venetians. And look how successful they were! If everyone has a genuine stake in society, and certain groups aren't made to feel marginalised, then the country will pull together instead of tearing itself apart. Of course it's a two-way thing."

"Precisely," said Angelo. "You know as well as I do that the biggest trouble-makers in Europe right now are the Muslims. They live among us, sure, but only because it suits them. Deep down they have no intention of integrating. They see our culture as 'haram'. Oh yes, Michelle, I have done my homework. The fact is, slowly but surely they are trying to change Western culture with their medieval beliefs. Their ultimate dream, as you and I both know, is to establish a European Caliphate. Well…

over my dead body!"

"Whilst I agree with most of what you say, I don't think it's as simple as that," said Michael, diplomatically. "It's not Muslims per se that are the problem. It's Islamists."

"You can split hairs if you want to. As far as I'm concerned they are two sides of the same coin. They will never, *ever,* integrate fully into Christian society. They are like a band of fifth columnists just waiting for the right moment to rise up. And rise up they will, mark my words, especially when you consider the birthrate of Muslims in Europe compared to that of Christians. Eventually sheer force of numbers will tip the balance. So it is not a question of 'when' or 'if'. It is simply a question of mathematics. And I read somewhere that Mohammad is now the most popular boy's name in the UK. So you see, the signs are already apparent — their insistence on serving Halal meat in our schools, their constant requests for setting up Sharia courts, not to mention the divisive way they dress and their constant sniping about the decadence of our society. A society, I might add, they are free to leave whenever they like. They know where the airport is."

"But surely the root of problem is the ruling elite: the lawmakers in our society who allowed this to happen in the first place."

Michael had hit a raw nerve.

Angelo stopped abruptly, folded his arms and gazed across the lake towards a mass of storm clouds gathering over the Alps. "I will personally march every single one of those faceless bureaucrats out of their nondescript offices, line them up against the wall and shoot them."

On the final evening of their three-day visit Angelo laid on a treat: dinner at The Kitchen in Como, a modern, ivy-clad Michelin star restaurant a stone's throw from the lake. After enjoying a glass of champagne in the magnificent *Sala di Mars,* the party made their way through the perfumed garden down to the private jetty where a sleek 1930's motor launch took them on the short journey to the critically-acclaimed eatery.

As soon as they entered, Angelo caused a stir, glad-handing the star-struck diners who burst into spontaneous applause. Michael saw at once how he commanded the room — flirting with the ladies, flattering the men — charming everyone present. In a bravura display of self-promotion he announced, in his musical voice, "*Signora e signori.* May I present my great friend Michael Taylor; the next Prime Minister of Great Britain. No doubt you've seen him on the news recently giving the British Government a bloody nose. He and I have been discussing the future of Europe."

"*Forza!*" shouted one of the diners, a petrochemicals bigwig.

"Indeed! And I can promise you this, like the phoenix from the ashes our two great nations will rise up and build a future we can all be proud of!"

The entire restaurant clapped, cheered and hammered on the tables.

Like Sadie's father David, Angelo Scarpi prided himself on his ability to predict the future; after all, it's what made him such a successful businessman and canny political operator. But even he couldn't have foreseen the momentous, game-changing event that took place the following morning as he and Claretta hosted a farewell breakfast for their British guests on the patio of *Palazzo Giallo*. He was just telling everyone about his recent purchase of a Serie A football club when the butler rushed out of the house and stood there ashen-faced.

"Goodness me!" said Angelo. "Don't tell me we've run out of coffee?"

"No, *dottore...*"

"Out with it then."

"It's just been announced on the news... King Charles has been assassinated."

The country Michael returned to was not the one he'd left. Just walking through the Arrival's Hall at Manchester Airport was enough to tell him that things had changed. There was something in the air. Something febrile. Royalist or not, the look on people's faces told him this was personal. What had taken place at the Migrant Processing Centre earlier in the day — when newly-arrived twenty-three-year-old Abbas Abdulla plunged a knife into HM King Charles III — went beyond the killing of a king. It was an attack on the very essence of British identity. Most would have laughed at such an idea, but there they were, people from all ethnic backgrounds and social classes, gathered around the TV inside Costa, shocked beyond words. Like a once in a millennium storm sweeping through the desert, the assassination had unearthed a magnificent, long-forgotten city, its streets, temples and arcades lying in ruins.

XVII

LYING ON HER STOMACH, dead to the world, Haley reached out and switched on the bedside fan. It took a few moments before the cool air swept across her naked body. She opened one eye and saw the results of last night's party — beer cans, gin bottles, empty cigarette packets, torn pages from her ever-present sketchbook — strewn across the bare concrete floor. She had a banging headache, made worse by the noise of the fish market across the street.

She'd come to Goa a month ago. 'Escaped' would be a better word. As soon as the general election was announced she told her boyfriend Saleem that they needed to 'get the fuck out'. "I don't want to see that man's face all over the media. It's bad enough as it is!"

It was Saleem who suggested Goa.

Rather than stay in the usual beachside resort popular with Europeans, they chose to rent a cheap backstreet flat in the fishing village of Arambol. Both she and Saleem were in their final year at Goldsmiths. Both had end-of-term Grad shows coming up. Neither was short of inspiration. Saleem was an environmental video artist; through his work he wanted to show the calamitous consequences of industrial fishing not only on the world's oceans, but on small, indigenous fishing communities. Haley's passion was the evils of colonialism and its legacy. So Arambol suited them perfectly.

While Saleem went out early each morning to document the lives of the fishermen and their families, Haley — sketch book in hand — explored the many towns and villages along the coast that were once part of the Portuguese Empire. Her goal was to produce a series of paintings that highlighted the marginalisation of indigenous communities and the destruction of their traditional culture.

Eventually Haley got out of bed and slid on a purple sarong she'd bought the previous day at the local market. Dying of thirst she opened the fridge, grabbed a bottle of water and gulped half of it down. Just then the door opened. Saleem stood there smirking.

"Well?" said Haley. "Hit me with it."

"I'm now the first member of my family to have slept with the daughter of a British prime minister."

"You're joking! The fucker got in! *Really!*"

Saleem noticed how angry she was, her blue eyes blazing. So he quickly moderated his tone, nodding gravely.

"'Fraid so… By a landslide."

"Oh my… Oh my *GOD!!!*" she screamed, pacing the room. She kicked the empty beer cans — "The bastard! The fucking *bastard!*" — sending them crashing against the wall. She went to the window and looked out; instead of the usual third-floor view of rooftops and glittering ocean, all she could see was her father standing on the doorstep of 10 Downing Street with that bitch Sadie posing for the press.

"Actually I think it's pretty cool," remarked Saleem, taking a beer from the fridge and fizzing it open.

Haley froze. "What?" She turned to look at her boyfriend standing there in his cute shorts and Megadeath T-shirt, his handsome face smeared in fish oil.

"I'm just saying, if it was *my* dad, hate him or not, I'd be pumped."

Pumped

She let the word sink in. "*PUMPED!* Are you out of your *fucking* mind! The man's a fascist!"

"Calm down, babes."

She set off pacing the room again. "Don't tell me to calm down, Saleem. Do *not* tell me to calm down!" She grabbed a hair tie off the dressing table. Pushing her apple-blonde hair through the elastic loop she continued to rant. "It's a disaster. A complete fucking disaster!"

"Dad doesn't think so. When I spoke to him just now he said there's a few demonstrations, but most people are happy."

"Happy!" She spat out the word as if it was poison. "You'll be telling me he voted for him next."

"Actually he did."

Sadie shook her head, exasperated. "I don't believe I'm hearing this! Why the *fuck* would a Muslim vote for someone who hates Muslims?!"

"Dad reckons that's bullshit, and that ordinary, law-abiding Muslims have got nothing to fear. He said it's about time someone got to grips with the extremists. Like he said, they're ruining it for everyone else."

"And then they came for me, Saleem. And then they came for me. Do you know who said that?"

"Donald Trump."

That was it. Sadie couldn't handle her laidback boyfriend's laidback attitude any longer; his annoying habit of making a joke out of everything. Didn't he realise how important this was to her? Couldn't he see how dangerous the result was for the UK? For the world? Obviously not, with such an inane comment.

She glared at him. "Right! I'm out of here!"

Flinging open the rattan wardrobe she pulled out her rucksack and started stuffing it with clothes.

"What are you doing?"

"What does it look like?"

"Seriously?"

"I'm not staying here one second longer."

"Come on Haley. Don't be silly." She carried on squashing her things into the rucksack, cursing under breath. "Haley!" Saleem walked over to her and put a calming hand on her shoulder. "Stop it. Please. Let's talk-"

"Get off!"

He removed his hand and stared at her contemptuously. "D'you know what I think?"

"I'm amazed you think at all, Saleem."

"The only reason you went out with me was because you thought it'd piss your dad off. "

Sadie snatched up her sketchbooks and threw the rucksack across her back. Ramming her feet into her flip-flops she headed for the door.

"Fuck you."

"Oh yes, very mature, I must say."

She flung it open, "*FUCK YOU!!*" slamming it behind her.

Saleem stood there for a moment, listening to her receding footsteps echo along the corridor. Weary after a hard morning at sea he sat on the bed and chugged down the rest of his beer. A huge weight seemed to lift from his shoulders. He smirked. "It is pretty cool though."

After her parent's divorce Haley changed her surname by deed poll — choosing Knight, her mother's maiden name — so there were no press waiting for her at Heathrow Airport. She was met by Lonny Kanz, a thirty-eight-year-old independent bookshop owner and leader of Direct Action, a left-wing fringe group he'd formed when GB Patriots were on the rise. Haley had first encountered Lonny in a pub close to Goldsmiths one night. Listening to him ranting about the need for violent revolution was a step too far for her at the time. Yes she believed in the same things he did, but not his methods. So she drank up and left.

All that changed when Michael became an

MP and GB Patriots started winning council seats. Horrified at her father's success and what it might mean for the country, she was desperate to join the opposition and throw her weight behind what she saw as a 'moral crusade.' She considered joining the Labour Party, but dismissed the idea — their recent lurch to the right in a cynical attempt to make them more electable was similar to what Tony Blair had done in the late 90s. To Haley that was a betrayal of the Labour Movement, of the brave men and women in the past who had shed blood for the party.

Disillusioned with the mainstream parties she began to investigate some of the many fringe groups that were starting to crop up. But her search proved useless; most of the ones she encountered were nothing more than glorified talking shops where people sat around naval-gazing. They were too moderate, too wishy-washy. She wanted action, not words. Then she remembered Lonny Kanz from the pub. His fiery, revolutionary rhetoric that had frightened her at the time suddenly made sense. So one lunchtime a few months before she went to Goa she popped into the pub to ask the landlord for Lonny's details. She eventually tracked him down to his Marxist bookshop in Hoxton.

Veritas was sandwiched between a dry cleaners and a kebab shop. A former nail salon, it was crammed from floor to ceiling with left-wing books and underground magazines. What little space there was taken up by a small table-cum-counter wedged into the corner, its surface covered in assorted paperbacks, anarchist pamphlets, used coffee mugs and scrunched up chocolate wrappers. Next to the counter was a battered Chesterfield where customers could read or simply hang out. While above, staring down benignly, was a faded black and white poster of Karl Marx.

The shop was empty at the time so naturally they fell into conversation about politics. Despite their age difference Haley found him fascinating. Lonny was the polar opposite of Saleem — short and chubby, with shoulder-length brown hair tied in a ponytail, he had absolutely no dress-sense whatsoever, which she found endearing. But what he lacked in looks he more than made up for in intellect. Here was a serious man who understood the world, who was sensitive to women's issues and saw through the racist veneer of Western Capitalism; the kind of man she was increasingly gravitating towards. What really attracted her was Lonny's passion for hands-on activism and his knowledge of all things political. He seemed to know everything! For instance, when she told him she was doing her Grad show on the theme of colonialism, he took her to the corner of the bookshop and pulled from the shelf half a dozen dog-eared books on the subject.

While she was deciding which one to buy he went into the back and made coffee. In the end she chose a book about the Mau Mau revolt in Kenya.

"Good choice," said Lonny, handing her a mug

stamped with the hammer and sickle. "Documents some of the atrocities we committed over there, all in the name of 'Empire'."

They sat for over an hour discussing the state of fascist Britain. She was surprised how shy and softly-spoken he was; so different from the firebrand she'd first encountered in the pub.

"That's why I set up Direct Action. It's time to make a stand."

"I couldn't agree more," she said, noticing how, unlike Saleem and the rest of the male students at Goldsmiths, he never once looked at her breasts.

Sitting in the cramped, musty bookshop discussing geopolitics as the rain hammered against the window, Haley felt right at home. It wasn't long before the subject of Michael Taylor came up.

Lonny was scathing, calling him a 'neo-Nazi' and a 'traitor to his race', someone who needed to be 'stopped at all costs'. Painful though it was to hear her father described in such terms, nevertheless Haley agreed, and before she left the bookshop she joined Direct Action.

Her first political demonstration was outside a GB Patriots rally in Leicester. She couldn't believe how big the venue was, and how many black and Asian people were attending. Standing behind a police cordon with anarchists and fellow anti-fascist groups — some wearing Guido Fawkes masks, others wrapped in bandanas — Haley chose not to hide her face. Lonny warned her beforehand to cover up as the police always filmed the demos. Ever the rebel, she ignored his advice and made a point of standing right at the front, secretly hoping it would get back to her father.

At first she kept her identity secret from Lonny, but when their friendship turned sexual she finally confessed. Straight away he saw similarities to Patty Hearst; the kidnapped American heiress turned gun-toting terrorist. She made him promise not to tell anyone, fearing the members of Direct Action would treat her differently. He vowed to keep his promise… for now anyway.

"I've split with Saleem," was the first thing she said when she got into his van outside Heathrow's Terminal 1.

"Thought as much when I got your text."

She loved the fact that, despite her new status (it was only a matter of time before she would be featured in newspapers and magazines) he was unshaven and wore his usual combat pants and scruffy black jumper; the polar opposite of her vain, immaculately-dressed father or fashion-obsessed ex.

"Is it OK if I crash at yours, Lonny? I need to sort my head out."

"Sure, no problem. Stay as long as you want."

She leaned across and kissed him on the cheek. "Thanks."

As he pulled out of the underground car park and sunlight flooded the van's interior, he noticed how six weeks under the Goan sun had supercharged Haley's natural beauty. Despite coming off a long flight and wearing zero makeup, her skin, toasted a deeper brown, shone with bronze-like intensity; her sparkling blue eyes, frizzy blonde hair, ripped jeans and faded Patti Smith T-shirt, the bangle of pink shells she wore on her wrist, all giving her the look of a beautiful beach bum. He couldn't believe the daughter of a British prime minister had flown half way across the globe to be with him.

Driving towards London, Haley looked out of the window at the depressing rows of identical semi-dethatched houses. She imagined what Saleem was doing at that moment — sitting at their favourite beach-side bar enjoying a cold beer; the dazzling blue sky, the turquoise ocean. Perhaps she'd been too hasty flying home?

No, fuck that!

"Can you believe we've got a fascist prime minister?" said Lonny, pulling onto the slip road.

"I know. My own father! I'm so ashamed."

"Don't be. We can't help our parents." He slammed his fist against the steering wheel. "What the *fuck* is wrong with black people in this country!? Fancy voting for a cunt like that! Can't they see where all this is gonna lead?" He wanted to see how far he could push it before her paternal loyalty kicked in.

"They've been brainwashed, Lonny. Pure and simple."

"Too right. Sheep the lot of them. Well, the

gloves are off. We need to organise. Take to the streets. We can't let this happen."

Swept up by Lonny's fervor she took hold of his hand. "It's great to be back."

"Perfect timing. The shit's about to hit the fan." He grabbed a Mars Bar off the dash and tossed it into her lap. Open that would you, Hale'. Not had any breakfast."

Before boarding the flight to London she had called her mother's house in Wilmslow. It was her new partner Ben who picked up. "Good timing. Your mum's just walked through the door."

"What took you so long to answer, Ben? I've been ringing for ages."

"The phone's not stopped since the election result. I've been ignoring it… Hang on. I'll just put her on… It's Haley."

"Hi, darling. How's Goa?" Her mother sounded weary.

"I'm about to fly home. Saleem and I have split up... Anyway never mind about Goa. Can you believe what's happened?! Dad! Prime *fucking* minister!"

Emma sighed. "Well, he's finally achieved his dream."

"How are you feeling?"

"Like you, it's hard to take in… I know this sounds odd, but in a funny sort of way I feel responsible."

"How!?"

"I remember having an argument with him one night about migrants crossing the Channel. He hadn't shut up about it for weeks. I was so fed up I turned to him and said, 'Put yourself up for election then, if it bothers you that much!' And he did. And look what's happened."

"It's hardly your fault, Mum."

"I know… It's some achievement though. I'll give him that."

Haley didn't like the warmth in her voice. "Don't say that! Dad treated you like shit." She remembered how cut-up her mother was after the split; the weekly train journeys up to Wilmslow every Friday to support her; the heartbreak, the tears. She hated her father after that. Hated him. "You're better off without him, Mum. He's a selfish prick with a giant ego. Always has been."

She had to confess though, when she saw the white cliffs of Dover from the aircraft window, and then the patchwork of fields, towns and villages scrolling beneath, her ego began to inflate (her father now ruled this land). And even though she would never admit it, when she landed at Heathrow and didn't see a single paparazzi waiting for her in the Arrival's Hall, she was well and truly pissed off, which shocked her somewhat.

XVIII

THE ATMOSPHERE inside the Commons was electric. Four hours after he first got to his feet David Yip gripped the side of the despatch box and proclaimed, "Madam Speaker, I commend this Budget to the House!"

Government MPs roared their approval — shouts, cheers, the waving of order papers. Directly across the chamber, the Opposition, their numbers decimated at the recent general election, shook their heads or simply stared at the floor. With a record 587 seats, GB Patriots had won the largest majority in Parliamentary history, beating the Conservative Party's 522 in 1931.

David Yip collapsed into his seat, his face drenched in sweat. Gulping down a glass of water he felt his shoulders peppered with congratulatory slaps.

Michael sat there beaming. Because of the noise in the Commons he had to shout in order to be heard. "Brilliant, David! Well done." His Chancellor had just delivered one of the most audacious budgets the House of Commons had ever witnessed; a modern-day Marshall Plan, a massive investment program that dwarfed anything gone before. True to their election promises, trillions of pounds of government money was to be spent renewing Britain's creaking infrastructure — road, rail, the NHS, a rollout of

Green energy projects, plus a special investment fund that would see the creation of a huge science and technology park in South Wales — Britain's Silicon Valley — that would attract some of the world's most talented scientists and AI companies. As each new detail was announced the Opposition grew more and more animated, demanding to know who would pay for all this largesse. "The same people who spent billions bailing out the banks during the last financial crisis," replied the Chancellor to one Conservative MP's point of order. "The British tax payer! Who, for once, will see a return on their investment, an investment that will improve the lives of every single one of our citizens in the form of a brand-new country."

But the biggest shock was left until the end; three major announcements that sent shockwaves through the Opposition benches — "During the next parliament this government will renationalise the Post Office, the railways and the steel industry, as well as scrapping the BBC license fee and completely reorganising the benefits system. All these measures announced today will make Britain the most modern, most forward-thinking country in the world. A country we can *all* be proud of… Madam Speaker, I commend this Budget to the House!"

Coupled with legislation laid out in the King's Speech during the State Opening of Parliament, which included abolishing the House of Lords and replacing it with a democratically-elected second chamber, the reintroduction of the death penalty for murder, and a mandatory thirty-year jail sentence for rape, key aspects of the government's strategy were now in place.

Top of the agenda was immigration: Michael's flagship policy. Overseeing its implementation was the Home Secretary, Grace Magars. As a former Border Force inspector she was put in charge of an entirely new organisation — the Department for National Security — one that was properly funded, with highly-trained and motivated staff whose remit was to protect Britain's borders. Within the DNS Grace created the Special Deportation Division, a nationwide force with offices in every major UK city tasked with locating, arresting and deporting a huge backlog of migrants who had entered the country illegally over the past two decades. To allow this process to run smoothly the government withdrew from the European Convention of Human Rights and passed legislation to curb the power of immigration lawyers.

On day-one of his administration Michael ordered the Royal Navy to increase its patrol of the English Channel and intercept the ever-increasing number of small boats run by people smugglers. Whereas in the past illegal migrants would be helped aboard Coast Guard vessels and taken to Dover, the Royal Navy was now ordered to attach a line to the boats and tow them back to the French beaches, much to the consternation of the Élysée Palace. But

Michael, along with the rest of the UK, had little sympathy with the French. For years their neighbours from across the Channel had received millions of pounds of British taxpayer's money promising to halt illegal crossings, when in reality they turned a blind eye. It was well known that France wanted rid of the migrants and secretly encouraged them to cross. Proof came in a series of photos printed in a national newspaper of French police standing idly by as a large dingy packed with migrants set out to cross the Channel.

So when the first boats were turned round and shepherded back to Normandy, the National Rally party seized on this, not only blaming the French government for its weak, ineffectual immigration policy, but praising Prime Minister Taylor for putting his citizens first. The strategy had been secretly agreed between the leaders of Europe's far-right parties during Michael's mini-summit on the Continent, which ended at the *Palazzo Giallo*. The plan was simple — if either of their parties got elected it would start sending migrants back to the country they first arrived from. This, they calculated, would cause a domino effect as outraged citizens from each of those countries demanded their government do the same. The chances of any European liberal administration agreeing to that were nonexistent, thus heralding a surge in popularity for the far-right. And that was exactly what was happening in France. As nightly news bulletins showed migrants clambering out of dinghies towed back to shore by the Royal Navy, National Rally's membership tripled overnight.

These specially designed patrol vessels — nicknamed 'Taylor's Tugboats' by *The Sun* newspaper — operated twenty-four hours a day, three hundred sixty-five days a year. Overnight the number of small boats reaching UK shores fell dramatically. And with increased beach patrols and a vast array of CCTV surveillance cameras set up along the coast, the few migrants who did get through were quickly rounded up, given a hot meal then immediately flown back to their country of origin on specially chartered aircraft.

After decades of inaction by previous governments the majority of citizens were right behind this radical new approach, relieved that at last something was being done to protect Britain's borders. Those who weren't took to the streets. A demonstration was held in Trafalgar Square where speaker after speaker condemned what was taking place, accusing the government of using 'Nazi tactics'. Outbreaks of violence by left-wing groups outside migrant detention centres became more frequent as they attempted to disrupt the deportations. Michael had expected this, so instructed Grace Magars to beef-up police numbers and increase the minimum jail term for those arrested. Initially the head of the Prison Service, Sir Roy Armstrong, was against these new measures, writing to the prime minister in the strongest possible terms, pointing out that British prisons were dangerously full already. But his attitude changed when it became apparent that, due to the large number of foreign criminals being deported on an almost daily basis, there was soon an excess of prison places.

A knock-on effect of the deportations, as Michael had predicted, was a massive saving in benefit payments and a freeing-up of social housing. It not only meant that more money was now available for vulnerable British claimants, it went a long way in solving the homeless crisis, as accommodation set aside by local authorities to house migrants was now accessible to British citizens living on the streets, which in turn saw a decrease in drugs offences and antisocial behavior.

Another of GB Patriots' policies was the complete transformation of the education system, starting with the universities. In Michael's eyes these so-called 'halls of learning' were nothing more than indoctrination centres run by leftist intellectuals aimed at turning young people against their own country. Ever since the 1960s, Marxist lecturers had insidiously planted seeds of self-loathing in their students. Britain's history and its culture, white heterosexual culture in particular, they deemed evil, oppressive, and racist in nature. It had to be torn down and destroyed. Only then, they said, could a new society be built, a society where everyone's needs would be catered for, not matter how outlandish. And the fact that former students of these propagandists were now in charge of major institutions such as the BBC and numerous government Think Tanks, proved the indoctrination had been a success.

Something had to be done to reverse this trend and restore patriotism in the young. The job was given to his Education Secretary and MP for Rochdale, Dr. Angela Murphy. Dr. Murphy was one of the UK's leading clinical psychologists, an expert in the study of herd mentality.

Angela relished the task, and was convinced she had the right strategy to solve the problem. As she explained to Michael when they met inside Number 10, "This is the first time in history that the younger generation have wanted the same thing as their parents — home ownership, a job for life, an index-linked pension — anathema to previous generations who, since time immemorial, have always rebelled against the status quo. The reason for this sudden volte-face is down to two things. Firstly, that children born to so-called 'Millennials' and 'Generation Z's were brought up to believe they were special. There was nothing they couldn't have. All they had to do was reach out a take it. It was their 'right'."

Michael smiled.

Umm. Just like Haley.

"What this did, Prime Minister, was produce a generation of self-entitled teenagers who believe they were special. So special, in fact, they were convinced the rest of the world was interested in their inner-most thoughts, no matter how facile. And they had the perfect outlet for this in the form of the newly-created World-Wide-Web. As the technology developed and more and more platforms opened up, teenagers flooded social media with 'selfies' and 'blogs', producing a plethora of 'likes' and 'smilies' from mums, dads and friends, bolstering their self-esteem.

"But it wasn't long before they came to the attention of internet 'Trolls' and cyber bullies, who tore into them, causing their fragile egos to crumble. And when it dawned on them that fame and fortune were mere illusions; that what they said, did or thought was of no consequence whatsoever, the generation who were told they could have it all retreated to their bedrooms where a deep-seated neurosis set in, triggering a host psychotic conditions — eating disorders, ADHD, body dysmorphia, gender issues, etc.

"So who was to blame for all this misery? Not them, obviously! It was society in general and their parents in particular for feeding them false dreams. And it's this generation, Michael, this 'Lost Generation,' the ones about to go to university, which we need to target. They're angry. And that anger is a good thing. It means they've regained the rebellious streak inherent in all teenagers. And we can that put to good use."

"How?"

"Disillusioned, they're desperately looking for

a cause of some sort to give their life meaning; something outside themselves; something that would differentiate them from their parents and older peers; something that would finally mark them out as 'special'."

"Which is?"

"Patriotism... If we can get our message across now, then once they get to university they will do our work for us."

"Brilliant, Angela. Get to it."

"I have to say, Michael, we're all *very* impressed at the way you're handling things on this side of the pond, both politically and socio-economically. Very impressed indeed."

"Thank you, Kirsty. It's not been plain sailing though."

"Yeah, I noticed the small group of protestors camped outside the gates as I drove in." She flashed her famous Louisiana smile. "You can please some of the people some of the time... Truth is, when all's said and done, the majority of the country is right behind you... I've seen your approval ratings. Eighty-nine percent. *Jeez!* Where I come from that's called shittin' in tall cotton."

Michael doubled up with laughter.

He was hosting a private dinner at Chequers for Kirsty McClane — the 49th President of the United States — who had flown over for a-meet-and-greet, their second since he became prime minister. He liked Kirsty from the moment they first met in Washington, her homespun Southern charm hiding a steely intellect. They were similar in age, which certainly helped matters. Although Kirsty was a die-hard Republican she was no female Donald Trump. She came from hard-working blue-collar parents. She was thoughtful, considered, with an honours degree in modern history from Harvard. Here was a woman he could do business with. Like Michael she understood the meaning of 'realpolitik', and not the wishy-washy, do-gooder liberal version that had cause so much trouble in the West over the years — interfering in other country's affairs, cack-handed attempts at nation-building. All that had done was breed resentment and make the world a more dangerous place.

"I'm flattered you've come to see me so soon," said Michael, as they ate dinner in the Jacobean wood-paneled dining room. No secret service agents. No special advisors. Just the two of them.

"Think nothing of it. Great Britain is our closest ally, and I wanna keep it that way… Besides, London's my favourite city." She leaned forward conspiratorially. "Please don't tell the French I said that."

Michael smirked. "Don't worry, your secret's safe with me. Although I'm sure you say the same about Paris when you're over there."

She leaned back in mock surprise. "Michael! *Really!* Are you suggesting I'm a cynical old politician?"

"Well, perhaps not old."

"Ooh! I'm gonna have to watch you! Yes sir!"

Relaxed atmosphere and pleasantries aside, they both had serious things to discuss, like the US's recent withdrawal from NATO, the ever-growing threat from China, and of course mass migration, both from the Middle East and Africa into Europe, and from Central America into the United States via Mexico. One of the reasons Kirsty had won the Presidential election was her tough stance on immigration, which under the Democrats and seen an alarming spike in numbers crossing the US's porous southern border.

President McClane had finally managed to complete Donald Trump's infamous 'wall', which dramatically cut the number of illegal crossings. And like Michael she was in the process of deporting those already in the US back to their homeland.

"Countries within the EU are slowly waking up to the disastrous open-door policy instigated by Angela Merkel," said Michael. He shook his head. "Madness. Sheer madness."

"Couldn't agree more. It was guilt, pure and simple, for Germany's treatment of the Jews during the Second World War. I mean, as if letting two million Muslims into your country can possibly erase that! You see, Michael, what people don't realise is, it's reckless policies like that that cause future holocausts."

"Umm, I hadn't thought of it that way."

"It's history repeating itself." She put her fork down and took a sip of champagne. "Ooh, that's nice..." she carried on her train-of-thought. "There's a line from a Woody Allen movie that illustrates my point — *Hanna and Her Sisters* I think it is — where one of the characters says… and I'm probably misquoting here, 'The shock isn't that the holocaust happened. Knowing what human beings are like, the shock is that it doesn't happen more often.'"

Michael stifled a laugh.

"That's what these bleeding-heart liberals don't understand: their naïve generosity will have serious consequences further down the line. That's why I'm glad to see your policy of turning those boats around in the English Channel seems to be working. More and more Europeans and are realising their respective governments made a huge mistake opening their borders allowing millions of people from different cultures to flood in; cultures that aren't exactly a fan of how we live in the West. I've noticed more and more EU citizens are turning their backs on their political masters and voting for right-wing parties, which can only be a good thing. Stop the problem before it starts, that's what I say."

"You're a breath of fresh air Kirsty, really you are… Now, I'd like to talk about your decision to withdraw from NATO. As you know, Russia is delighted. Is there any chance I can persuade you to reconsider?"

"*Ah-ha! Now* I know why were drinking Pol Roger." She glanced at the champagne resting in the silver ice bucket. "That wouldn't be one of the famous bottles laid down by Churchill during the Second World War, would it?" She lifted the dripping bottle and read the label, gasping in mock surprise, "Why of *course* it is! And a 1943 vintage at that!" She shot him a wry smile. "You're a scoundrel, Michael. You know how much I admire Winston Churchill. Shame on you, trying to bribe a lady."

Michael threw up his hands. "Mea culpa, Madam President. Mea culpa. Then you'll appreciate his famous quote: 'Champagne is the wine of civilisation and the oil of government.'"

"Not in this case it ain't. Fact is, the US taxpayer is sick of spending trillions of dollars defending Europe when those self-same governments keep cutting back on their defence budgets. We just can't afford it anymore." She noticed Michael was about to jump in. "However, I'm not referring to Great Britain here. You guys have always paid your way, and the fact that you've recently increased your defence spending has allowed me some leeway. So what I'm proposing is, a joint defence treaty; something along the lines of, if Russia or China attacks then the US will come to your aid… And if, in time, the rest of Europe follows Britain's example, maybe I'll reconsider."

The next morning they returned to London. In the afternoon, before flying back to Washington, Kirsty and Michael signed the 'Special Defence

Agreement' in front of the world's press, adding an extra layer of mortar to the Special Relationship.

XIX

SADIE AND MICHAEL were having breakfast in their newly renovated flat above Number 10; although the term 'flat' no longer applied. Both Number 10 and Number 11 had been combined into a spacious apartment similar to their Alderley Edge penthouse.

Sadie had taken charge of the renovation, ordering the workmen to remove the old-fashioned fixtures and fittings to create a clean, bright, fashionable home fit for a 21st century prime minister.

A few days after the renovations were complete she invited Akshata Murty, wife of Rishi Sunak, over for lunch. Akshata couldn't believe the change. She was amazed at the transformation, confessing she had always wanted to give the place a makeover but had been advised against it due to government cutbacks. Sadie assured her that those days were gone.

It was true. Number 10 was now a microcosm of what was taking place across the length and breadth of the United Kingdom. With trillions of pounds at Michael's disposal courtesy of the IMF, the country was slowly being transformed into a gleaming high-tech jewel. Brand-new hospitals, schools, major road and rail projects — including HS3, a line from London to Edinburgh — plus a massive council-house building program not seen since the 1950s, meant unemployment figures were at a record low. And all those on the left who had raged against Michael's immigration and deportation policies, predicting that work on these 'vanity projects' would soon grind to a halt due to manpower shortages, were shocked when the government handed out thousands of visas to skilled workers from all parts of the globe. True to his word, if you met the new criteria and wanted to contribute to UK society, you were welcomed into the country, a country that looked to the future with a renewed sense of optimism, a country at ease with itself.

An unashamed sense of patriotism permeated all classes of society, a kind of 'let's all pull together' ideal not seen since the dark days of the Second World War. The existential angst had gone. Once again people took pride in celebrating their Britishness — a completely new concept to the younger generation brought up to revile the nation's history — the coronation of King William III its apotheosis.

The royal jamboree was held in September. Michael declared a four-day national holiday. Sales of Union Flags soared. People up and down the land took pride in decorating their villages, towns and cities. As world leaders and crowned heads flew into Britain for the coronation at Westminster Abbey, street parties and bonfires were organised all across the UK. On the day itself the capital was bathed in autumnal sunshine. The night before, aware their city would be the focus of world attention, hundreds of young people from London's inner-city communities volunteered to pick litter and tidy the streets — Muslims, Christians, Hindus, Sikhs. At precisely 12 p.m. the crown was lowered onto the head of King William, signaling scenes of unbridled joy.

After almost a year in power Michael's administration had radically altered the social landscape of the UK. With the Thought Police no longer around, people were free to express themselves without the fear of being 'cancelled' or judged.

As well as boosting the economy, another of Michael's popular initiatives was a crackdown on Islamic fundamentalism. Scores of Madrasas, mosques and Islamic schools suspected of spreading hate had been closed, their teachers and supporters deported, causing outrage across the Islamic World. To counter this, Michael appeared on Al Jazeera arguing that Britain was a tolerant country, home to all races and religions. What it wouldn't tolerate however, were hate preachers and people who hid behind their citizenship to undermine the country and plan acts of terrorism. These people might have got away with it in the past, but not now. After the interview, the reporter and his camera crew travelled to Leicester to interview a cross-section of the Muslim population. The vast majority supported the measures being taken, openly stating that only radical Islamamists and criminals were being deported, which vastly improved cross-community relations.

"I've never got on better with my Christian neighbours," said one Pakistani market trader.

The judiciary had also been reformed. Liberal judges, those who were viewed by the Home Secretary as being 'soft on crime', were replaced by hardliners. Consequently the amount of custodial sentences increased, as did the actual time criminals spent in prison. Twenty years meant twenty years, not ten, or eight. Strict new laws were put into place to deal with sex offenders, foreign grooming gangs in particular. Gone were the days when police were fearful of investigating such cases at the risk of upsetting 'cultural sensibilities'. Free from the shackles of political correctness, the police now prosecuted with zeal. Anyone found guilty of such a heinous crime, no matter how long they had lived in the country, whether they had come here as a child, even if they were married and had children, made no difference. They were immediately deported. Those who were born here were treated like everyone else — they were given a mandatory twenty year prison sentence with no chance of parole.

Unlike in the past, when such patriotic polices would have caused chest-beating outrage from the liberal media, opposition voices had sunk to a whisper. The head of the snake, as far as Michael was concerned, had been well and truly neutralised. As well as scrapping the licence fee — which was overwhelmingly popular — the BBC had undergone a complete restructuring from senior management downwards. Along with a brand-new code of ethics, a new vetting process was implemented, one that weeded out what the Home Secretary termed 'negative elements'. The result was uproar, triggering mass resignations from left-leaning commentators, presenters and journalists. Michael couldn't have wished for a better result. As he explained to his Secretary of State for Culture, Media and Sport, Christopher Juma — a former Great Britain Olympic 10,000 meters runner of Kenyan decent — "They've not only saved the corporation millions in overblown salary payments, people are no longer being told what to think."

Christopher laughed. "I know what you mean. It's a pleasure to switch the BBC on and not be preached at the whole time. No more left-wing presenters pointing accusatory fingers at the British public for their ancestor's role in the slave trade. No more guilt-ridden exposes calling out 'white privilege'. The BBC must have been the only state broadcaster in the world that talked down to the very people who funded it."

"I know," said Michael. "Unbelievable, isn't it."

"Thank God those days are gone and we can get on with building for the future."

Then a strange thing happened; without any prompting from government, Michael's photograph began to appear in banks, offices, schools, factories and shops. Some of his most ardent admirers even had a photo of him in their home. No other prime minister had been so idolised.

Michael got up from the breakfast table. He kissed Sadie goodbye, left the apartment and walked down the stairs past the descending line of former prime ministers' photographs. When he got into the hall the front door was already open. He could see the official car waiting to take him to Buckingham Palace for his regular Tuesday-morning meeting with the king. His official bodyguard, Reg, a former Royal Marine, was standing by the rear passenger door as usual, his eyes scanning left and right.

Emerging into the sunlight Michael heard shouts from the press pack on the far side of Downing Street.

"What do think of the situation in Europe, Prime Minister?"

"Are we getting involved?"

"What about all the protests this weekend?"

Michael gave his usual non-committal smile. Then, just as he was getting into the car, he heard, buried within the hastily shouted questions…

"Did you know your daughter is associating with a radical group of Marxists?"

Straight away Michael recognised the voice — Simon Mosley, an investigative reporter for the *Guardian* newspaper. His smile instantly vanished; but he was already inside the car so it wasn't noticed. Pulling out of Downing Street he let out a sigh of frustration. Of course he knew about his daughter;

the security services had told him months ago, showing him photos and video footage of her taking part in left-wing protests around migrant detention centres. It was only a matter of time before this came to light. And by the look of things it was about to. He had tried to make contacted with Haley several times via her mother, but Emma made it crystal clear that their daughter wanted nothing more to do with him. He knew where she lived, knew everything about her — the scruffy flat above a Marxist bookshop; the fact she shared a bed with Lonny Kanz, founder of Direct Action. Judging by what the security services told him, Kanz had previous convictions for violent affray and drug offences, so was about as unsavory as it gets.

Michael smashed his fist onto the rear passenger seat. Thinking a shot had been fired Reg spun round.

"Sorry, Reg."

Why wasn't Haley more like her twin brother Richard, who openly supported GB Patriots and was on friendly terms with Sadie? Why was she so … so ... *bloody minded?* She'd always been like that, ever since she was a child. He remembered when Haley was at nursery school and the head teacher called him in for a serious talk. Apparently she'd come to the aid of a Chinese boy who was being bullied in the playground. While Richard stood idly by watching, she ran over and attacked the gang of bullies, hitting them with her lunch box. It was the first in a series of such incidents that peppered her formative years, culminating in her getting expelled from one of Cheshire's most prestigious girl's schools. A born troublemaker, was how the head teacher described her. Wasn't *that* the truth! To think his darling daughter, his favourite, had shacked up with some Marxist radical.

Where did we wrong? We gave her everything. Everything! And look how she's turned out. She didn't even want me to attend her graduation.

Michael's day was about to get a whole lot worse. Rounding Admiralty Arch about to enter the Mall, a small group of protesters pelted his limousine with eggs, splattering the windscreen and bodywork. For a split second he thought he saw Haley standing amongst them, but he was he wrong.

"I'd go through the car wash on your way back if I were you," joked King William, as they both took a seat in the Audience Room. "I saw your car from the window. They made a right mess of it, I must say... Actually, the way the country is at the moment I'm surprised there are any protests at all."

"I'm not sure about that. There are two large anti-government demonstrations taking place this weekend; one in London, the other in Manchester."

"Well, you can't have it all your own way."

"True."

"Now, about the situation in Europe… All the riots taking place. And now that terrorist incident on the Paris Metro this morning. What more do we know?"

"Someone threw a grenade into one of the carriages, killing eighteen people… Islamic State has claimed responsibility."

"I see."

"I'm afraid the situation has escalated since then. I was informed by the French interior minister on my way here that a vigilante group burst into a school in Lyon an hour ago and shot five Muslim pupils."

William gasped. "Good God. Where will it all end?"

"As you're aware the French are going to the polls next week, so we'll know soon enough."

"After what's happened today it's a foregone conclusion, isn't it?"

"What? National Rally coming to power?" Michael shrugged. "Personally I think it's about time the French elected a government that will put its people first. Look where all this multiculturalism's got them."

As the king surmised, the following week France elected the National Rally by a huge majority, its combative leader promising to restore law and order. She was as good as her word. After eight straight days of rioting, troops were sent onto the streets to calm the situation. The radical changes she promised began the very next day. Two new laws were passed in the French parliament; the first was immediate withdrawal from the European Union; the second was to deport the thousands of migrants who had entered the country unlawfully. Large coordinated raids took place across the whole of France, arresting migrants and dismantling squatter's camps. Copying what the British had done, bus load after bus load were sent back across the border to Germany and Italy. PARIS EST LIBRE read the headline in one of the right-wing dailies, as it celebrated the removal of hundreds of unsightly tents that had cluttered the famous boulevards for the past decade, causing Parisians and tourists untold misery. 'We now have our glorious capital back', proclaimed the editorial: 'the romantic City of Lights. Soon lovers will be able to stroll unmolested through our beautifully-kept parks and streets without the fear of being robbed or sexually assaulted. Yet none of this would have come to pass if it hadn't been for the brave and farsighted immigration policy first brought about by our esteemed neighbour Prime Minister Michael Taylor; a modern-day Winston Churchill. Once again Britain has come to France's aid during her hour of need. Vive la Grande-Bretagne! Vive le France!'

The domino effect Michael had discussed with Angelo Scarpi on the banks of Lake Como was coming to pass. Italy and Germany were now awash with recently returned migrants, sending their respective citizens out onto the streets. As the European Parliament tied itself up in knots discussing how best to deal with the emergency, more and more people threw their support behind right-wing parties. Both populations had differing ways of protesting. In Germany, large, well-organised rallies were held in Berlin, Munich and Hamburg. As for the Italians; what started out as a series of peaceful demonstrations in Rome and Milan soon turned violent, with cars, buses and trams set on fire and public buildings ransacked. Cometh the hour, cometh the man.

Addressing a huge, highly-agitated crowd in Milan's main square, the entire stage bedecked in Italian national flags, Angelo Scarpi, wearing an immaculate dark blue suit, strutted up and down shouting bellicose statements mocking the European Parliament. Pointing in the general direction of Strasbourg, "a place of little consequence somewhere over the Alps," he let rip, "That rabble! That glorified talking shop, who, let us not forget, allowed these migrants to flood in in the first place, are now at a loss about how to deal with the situation, a situation they themselves created… People of Italy; we are being invaded. Yes, invaded! If we don't act now, and act with lightening speed, then Italy as we know it will come to an end."

The whole crowd in Piazza del Duomo roared its approval.

Intoxicated by the response, Angelo puffed out his chest, folded his arms and nodded his head in total agreement with himself. He gave the crowd its head before bringing it to heel with a raised hand. Ever the chameleon, he took a leaf straight out his good friend Prime Minister Taylor's political playbook.

As the crowd quietened, he strolled up and down the stage, peering at the many faces staring up at him. "As I look at this glorious crowd gathered here today, I'm heartened to see so many black, Arab and Chinese citizens — citizens whose forefathers settled here many years ago; citizens who have contributed a great deal to our society, enriching our culture in the process. So don't let the Left fool you into thinking my party is for white Italians only. It is not. It is for *all* patriotic citizens who are legally entitled to live in our beautiful land, who support the common good and want only what is best for the Italian nation! *FORZA ITALIA!!!*"

"*Haley!* Quick! Look at this!... Fuck me!"

Haley was in the basement painting when Lonny called out. She dropped her palette knife and dashed up the stairs.

Lonny was sitting bolt-upright on the sofa pointing at the TV, a look of disbelief on his chubby, unshaven face.

"It's started."

Haley stared at the television — thousands of demonstrators, some carrying anti-immigrant placards, others holding the German flag, were streaming through the Brandenburg Gate in Berlin.

"Oh my God…"

"It's just like the Brownshirts!" Lonny jumped up. "I knew this would happen. Knew it. That's what you get when you—"

"Shush!"

The camera had switched to a makeshift stage in front of the Reichstag. Flanked by officials, Hans Schuster, leader of the far-right Alternative for Germany Party, was addressing the crowd. Pointing at the building behind him he launched into a ferocious tirade against the liberal gangsters who ran the country. They had, he said, sold the German people down the river with their cloud-cuckoo-land-multicultural-polices. Inspired by the example set by Britain and France, he called upon all patriotic Germans to rise up and demand a general election. "Let the people decide who lives in this great Fatherland of ours!"

Haley slumped down next to Lonny and burst into tears. She put her head in her hands, rocking back and forth. "Oh God… What's he done... The fucking bastard!"

Lonny put his arm around her shoulders. "Don't get mad, Hale. Get even. There's lots of people who think like us."

"Let's organise a demo then. Take to the streets."

"We've tried that. Fat lot of good it's done. The fascists need to know we're not gonna take this lying down."

"What? Violence?"

"They've left us with no choice."

Haley shrunk back. "Oh no, Lonny, we can't do that."

"We *have* to! For fuck's sake look what's happening! People are being deported. Locked away without a proper trail. It won't be long before concentration camps are up and running!"

"Don't say that!"

"Why not? The entire media's brainwashing people with right-wing propaganda, especially the shit pumped out by the BBC. Where are all the free-thinkers? They've been silenced good and proper. People are frightened to open their mouths anymore."

Haley got up and walked to the window. "I know, I know."

"Well then? We can't just sit back. We have to do *something!*"

"Like what?"

XX

THE TWO ANTI-GOVERNMENT rallies that took place in London and Manchester both descended into violence, the London demonstration in particular. The capital had seen nothing like it since the Poll Tax riots in 1990. There were running battles with the police, shops were looted, public buildings defaced, buses and cars hijacked and set on fire. Things got so out of hand the Home Secretary ordered the army onto the streets. Hundreds of demonstrators were rounded up, put into trucks and taken to specially-built 'holding facilities' outside London. During one violent encounter in Whitehall, as demonstrators tried to break down the security gates at the entrance to Downing Street, Ajeet Sing, a forty-two-year-old sergeant in the Metropolitan Police, was knocked to the ground and stabbed to death. A devout Sikh, he left behind a wife and two children. Due to the number of CCTV cameras in the area his three murderers were soon identified and arrested: Alex Ross, Peter Castle and Julie Wilson: students from the London School of Economics.

The brutal murder of Sergeant Sing shocked the nation. Michael was so appalled he immediately suspended all forms of public demonstrations for the foreseeable future, angering constitutional experts. The next day he visited Govind Sing's widow.

Television cameras were there to record the prime minster taking tea with Mrs. Sing and her children in the lounge of their family home in Wembley. Later that evening he addressed the nation from the Cabinet Office in Number 10, where he announced that Sergeant Sing would receive a state funeral. This tragic event, he said, had made him more determined than ever to restore law and order and bring a sense of calm back to the nation. He would not, he went on, be intimidated by left-wing thugs. He promised to fight fire with fire, purging the nation of 'dark forces'. He would crack down hard on all those who were arrested so as to deter anyone foolish enough to repeat their actions. Although no details were given as to what form the 'crackdown' would take, he ended the address by saying…

"And to those cowards who murdered Sergeant Sing — a proud patriot who had served his country loyally for over twenty years — if found guilty they will receive the death penalty… Good night. And God save the king."

Haley was suspicious of the man as soon as he walked in; the awkward way he scanned the bookshelves without really looking; the way his eyes kept darting towards her as he strolled around the shop; his clothes, his hair. He just didn't seem right.

"Looking for anything in particular?"

"No, no, just erm…"

Fuck me! It's the security services!

"Lonny!"

Lonny came in from the back munching a piece of toast. Haley motioned at the man. Straight away Lonny's suspicion was aroused.

"Can I help you, mate?"

Realising his cover was blown he came out from behind one of the shelves and walked towards the counter smirking. "Wouldn't be much use as a secret agent, eh?"

"What do you want?"

"You're Haley Knight, aren't you: Michael Taylor's daughter?"

The hairs on the back of her neck stood on end. She knew this day would come.

"What's it got to do with you?"

"I'm Simon Mosley. I'm an investigative journalist for the *Guardian*."

"A reporter! Get the fuck out."

Confused, Simon glanced at Lonny, who immediately looked at the floor.

"What's going on Lonny? Do you know the guy?"

"Sort of."

"Sort of!"

"Just listen to what he has to say, Hale."

"Fuck me! What've you done?"

Simon tried to calm things. "I want do an in-depth interview with you, Haley. Give people your side of the story. It would really help the opposition. I mean, you're obviously not a fan of your father."

Raging, Haley stared at Lonny — "How *could* you!" — before storming into the back, crashing through the beaded curtain.

He told Simon to stay where he was and quickly followed. Haley was marching up and down shaking her head. "You promised you wouldn't say anything. *You promised!*"

"I know, but—"

"No buts, Lonny! You lied to me!"

Lonny hung his head.

"Don't act the innocent. How much is he paying you?"

That stung. "Now hang on a minute! I'm not doing this for the money. I don't give a shit about money."

"You betrayed me, Lonny. Simple as."

"Listen to you, Miss High and Fucking Mighty! If you must know, Simon's the only person I've told. I did it because—"

"Oh! You've only told a *'journalist'!* That's alright then—"

"Just listen for once in your life! This isn't about you! Look what's happening out there. In case you haven't noticed we're living in a fascist state. We need something, *anything*, that's gonna help the cause." He fixed her with a quizzical stare. "You *do* wanna help the cause, don't you? I mean, you're not just here for the pose?"

Ouch.

"Course I wanna help! How can you even *say*

that!?"

"Well then… This is your chance… You've told me a thousand times how much you hate your dad. What he stands for. What a bastard he was to your mum. Tell Simon. Tell the world." Her contrite body language told him she'd started to crumble. It was time for good cop. Always works. He went over and put his arm around her shoulders. "Think about it, Hale'. Think of the damage you could do. You'll be a hero to the anti-fascist movement."

Simon was flicking through a book about the Red Brigade when Haley reappeared through the beaded curtain.

"OK, Simon. Let's do it."

Emerging from the crystal waters of the Aegean, Michael swam to the rear of the *Mamma Rosa* — Angelo Scarpi's luxury yacht — and climbed onto the lowered platform. He'd been in the water for some time trying to come to terms with the excoriating article published that day in *Guardian* newspaper. Under the headline, THE REAL MICHAEL TAYLOR, it was Haley's account of her childhood. She ripped into Michael — his old-fashioned, bigoted views, his selfishness, the utter disdain in the way he treated his wife, his terrifying mood swings. 'Don't be fooled. Underneath all that charm is a raging narcissist who absolutely *has* to get his own way. And if he doesn't, watch out.'

That hurt. That really hurt. It was a character

assassination, pure and simple.

"Hi, sexy."

Michael took off his mask and squinted into the sun. Sadie was leaning over the guard rail wearing a bright yellow bikini; fresh from a massage she looked radiant, every inch the sun-kissed beauty.

"Look who's talking."

She scanned her boyfriend's muscular body. "Hey, nice tan… Oh God, was that racist?"

Michael put the article to the back of his mind, stood up and smirked. "Not anymore… I'm glad to say."

He climbed onto the deck. Sadie wrapped her arms around his waist, pressing herself against his wet skin. "Umm. Fresh from the sea."

He kissed her on the lips.

Suddenly, from off the port bow, came the ripping sound of camera shutters. Michael turned to see the ever-present line of power boats that had been shadowing the *Mamma Rosa* for the past two days.

Sadie tutted. "Fucking Paps!"

Michael was taking a short break before his official visit to Berlin where he was due to hold talks with the German Chancellor. Accepting an invitation from Signore Scarpi he and Sadie had flown by private jet to Kefalonia, boarding the *Mamma Rosa* shortly after landing. Angelo had bought the 120 meter super yacht from a cash-strapped Russian oligarch following the latest round of UN sanctions. Originally called the *Christina*, he'd renamed it after his beloved mother.

The flamboyant Italian was playing host to the leaders of Europe's far-right parties. With elections due in Italy, Germany and Sweden later that summer, they were keen to discuss strategy and liaise with their guest of honour, Prime Minister Taylor. Buoyed by the recent election results in France, which saw National Rally sweep to power, the group were hoping to celebrate with Madam le President herself. Unfortunately she couldn't join them due to civil unrest, but sent her best wishes and promised to attend the next meeting, which Michael was kindly hosting later in the year at Plumley Old Hall — a forty acre estate in the heart of the Cheshire countryside that Sadie's father had recently gifted to the couple.

The group had spent the morning discussing their vision for a new Europe, a Europe free from the bureaucratic tentacles of Brussels. The leader of Vlamms Belang, whose country was considered the *de facto* capital of the European Union, was scathing, telling everyone how he longed for the day when he would close down that 'talking shop' and turn the building into a centre for European culture, each room brimming with supreme masterpieces. "The message would ring out loud and clear — we are no longer ashamed of our culture. On the contrary, we are proud of it! But what I'm *really* looking forward to is sacking those overpaid, unelected technocrats, who for decades have issued diktat after diktat with little thought of how it affects ordinary people, and make them work for a living. Real work, not sitting on their padded backsides in some air-conditioned office. A good long spell in a factory will do them good. Show them what real life is all about! And for those who are physically unfit; those who have grown fat on their vast salaries and outrageous expense accounts — the majority in other words — I have a special treat in store: they will work in Belgium's newly-created Deportation Bureau, escorting migrants out of the country."

Laughter echoed round the room.

"Oh the irony!" shouted Angelo Scarpi. He got to his feet and began pacing the conference room, a long, teak-paneled salon formerly used as a bowling alley by the Oligarch's teenage son. "I for one am ashamed of what Europe has become — an homogeonised septic tank, a dumping ground for every conceivable race and creed; a vast reservoir of cheap labour for the multinationals to drawn upon, driving down the wages of our own citizens in the process. And they expect us to take that lying down? I think not."

Julia Teuling, the thirty-two-year-old straight-talking leader of Holland's Party for Freedom, took the baton. "Signore Scarpi is correct. We have been the victims of a monstrous experiment carried out by left-wing political scientists hell bent on destroying our culture. We are all aware of the 'Kalergi Plan' are we not: the ethnocide of the peoples of Europe through the encouragement of mass, non-white immigration, especially from Muslin countries... Well, not while I have breath left in my body. I want to see our continent return to a brotherhood of individual states, each one proud of its own values, peoples and traditions. After all, Sweden is not Italy, and France is not Greece, despite what Brussels has been telling us all these years. So let us follow the glorious example of Michael here, who has turned the United Kingdom into a land where people are no longer ashamed of their identity."

"Here! Here!"

There was fierce hammering on the table. Michael acknowledged each of the leaders with a modest nod of the head.

'*Raging narcissist*' He just couldn't get his daughter's article out of his mind.

Energised, Hans Schuster then added his own particular vision. "The day Alternative for Germany comes to power I will clear the Reichstag of all bleeding-heart liberals and pseudo-multiculturalists… I say 'pseudo', as none of them actually mix with the migrants they so willingly encouraged to come to Germany, making our citizens lives a misery in the process. How could they; they live in exclusive parts of Berlin and dine at Michelin star restaurants." He glanced around the conference table, nodding his head vigorously. "Oh yes, I am very much looking forward to dealing with *those* people."

The unofficial get-together ended with Angelo Scarpi throwing a magnificent banquet on the top deck of the *Mamma Rosa*. As the sun began to set and the sleek, polished craft cruised through the wine-dark sea, the leader of Niki, the largest of Greece's far-right parties, pointed to a small island off the starboard bow, informing his fellow diners proudly, "That, ladies and gentlemen, is Ithaca; ancient birthplace of Odysseus."

Michael gazed at the historic island, an ever-deepening blue mass in the Aegean twilight, mysterious and awe-inspiring. "I remember reading *The Odyssey* at school. I was obsessed... Another masterpiece Europe can be proud of." Looking round the dining table a shiver went down his spine; he could have been the man himself, leading his followers home from Troy.

The next day Michael flew to Berlin. While he was in the air he was informed by the Home Secretary that the three young students who'd murdered Sergeant Sing had been hung in the grounds of Belmarsh high security prison.

"It shows you mean business, Michael," said Grace, worried by the silence on the other end of the line.

"Yes I suppose it does... What's the mood of the country this morning?"

"Oh, the usual suspects have taken to the streets."

"No surprise there."

"The rest of the population are fine. The public

have wanted the restoration of the death penalty for years."

Landing at Brandenburg Airport he was met by the German Foreign Minister, Herr Schroder, an officious, taciturn man in his late sixties. The welcome was underwhelming to say the least; a cold shake of the hand and perfunctory "*Guten Tag.*" The reason became all too clear the moment they entered Berlin. Approaching the Reichstag the streets were lined with people of all ages cheering as they went by. Some waved Union Jacks, others the German national flag. Some even threw flowers. The look on Herr Schroder's face said it all — his government's days were numbered.

Michael waved at the passing crowds. Aware that a TV news crew had been following them since they left the airport, he tapped the driver on the shoulder. "Stop please."

The car slowed, pulling up next to the curb.

"No, no. We really haven't time," protested Herr Schroder, realising Michael's cheap publicity stunt would further destabilise his already unpopular administration.

"This won't take a minute."

Before the driver could react Michael jumped out of the car and plunged into the crowd. Sensing an exclusive, the TV news crew swung into action, leaping from the people carrier.

A massive cheer went up as Berliner's of all ages surrounded the British prime minister. Shouts of

"*Retter Europas!*" "*Retter Europas!*" (Savior of Europe) went up, along with good-natured cries of "*Bitte seien Sie unser Kanzler*" (Please be our Chancellor).

Sadie watched from inside the official limousine as Michael shook hands, accepted kisses and posed for selfies with the adoring crowd.

One minute turned into five. Enraged, Herr Schroder leaned over the front seat and blasted the horn. To his utter dismay he was caught on camera. After a minute or so more Michael tore himself away and got back into the car.

"Sorry about that. Got carried away."

The limousine finally set off. Herr Schroder was furious. "All this nationalism sweeping Europe is a dangerous thing."

"Who for?" asked Michael, michievously.

Soon they were driving through the entrance gates of the *Schloss Bellevue*, the Chancellor's official residence. The present incumbent, Herr Meier, was equally as cold. During informal talks outlining the proposed trade agreement between their two nations, he suddenly went off-track, accusing Michael of wrecking the European Union with his 'ill-conceived deportation policy that had flooded his country with thousands of migrants, causing social unrest.'

Michael could hardly believe what he was hearing. "It was your predecessor Angela Merkel who did that."

If the reception from the German government was downright chilly, the reaction of ordinary

Berliners couldn't have been warmer. As Michael was staying at the British Embassy on *Wilhelmstrasse*, a large crowd had gathered outside hoping to catch a glimpse of the great man and his glamorous partner. They got their wish later that evening when the ambassador took Michael and Sadie to the three Michelin star *Rutz*, Berlin's most exclusive restaurant.

An hour before, while he was showering, Sadie called him into the bedroom and pointed at the TV.

"Look Michael… The people love you."

Wrapped in a fluffy white towel he stared at the news footage of his impromptu walkabout — there he was, in the shadow of the Brandenburg Gate, surrounded by adoring crowds straining to touch him as though he were a rock star.

"*Retter Europas*!" they chanted … *Savior of Europe…*

He let the words sink in. He saw himself walking back to the official limousine. The camera then focused on a beautiful young *Fräulein* in the crowd, her alabaster complexion, long blonde hair and piercing blue eyes. Overcome with emotion she was smiling and crying at the same time.

He saw the effect he was having on the crowd; the joy, the adulation... *Savior of Europe…* Michael stood stock-still, water dripping from his face.

Beneath his towel he felt himself getting hard.

PART II

Which Side Are You On?

XXI

IN THE FOUR YEARS SINCE GB Patriots had come to power the UK had changed beyond recognition. Following the assassination of King Charles, Michael had single-handedly pulled the country up by its bootstraps, culturally, socially, and economically. With a booming economy, clean, peaceful streets, freedom of expression, a fully-functioning NHS, a transportation system that was the envy of the world, and the mass deportation of illegal migrants, the government was riding high in the opinion polls. Ordinary people could now openly display their patriotism without fear of being judged. On the contrary, showing one's patriotism was now considered 'fashionable', especially amongst the young, who had rebelled against what they considered to be their parent's 'selfish, unpatriotic values'.

The 'me me me' generation was well and truly under threat; Michael's Education Secretary Angela Murphy had seen to that. From primary school upwards — where the National Anthem was sung every morning at assembly — loyalty to one's country was not only nurtured but encouraged and sustained. Gone were the days when teachers and university lecturers hammered home guilt-ridden critiques of Britain and its history to their students, teaching them to respect every culture but their own. Now 'Britishness' was not only celebrated but openly displayed across all sectors of society — arts, entertainment, sport.

Proof of this came when a new crop of England players pulled on their shirts for an international against Brazil at Wembley Stadium. During the National Anthem, the younger members of the squad — a rainbow mix of different ethnic backgrounds — gripped their badges tightly, closed their eyes and sang with a passion never before seen on an English the football field, putting to shame the older members of the squad who, as usual, remained silent or mouthed the words with barely disguised contempt.

Turn on the TV and yet more examples could be found. Shows like the Black Music Awards and the Asian Music Awards were renamed the British Music Awards, each style and category — rock, soul, R&B, hip-hop, bangra etc — assessed on their own merits rather than racial bias, as was the case in the past. In fact the terms 'black', 'white', 'brown' etc were becoming less and less applicable as young people felt more at ease referring to themselves as simply 'British'.

It was only through the younger generation, Michael realised, that true and lasting change can occur. Of course there were voices of dissent. This is where things took a surreal turn. The Left suddenly found themselves in bed with the old-fashioned bigots who wanted to return to the days when people were categorised in terms of race and ethnicity, which caused howls of laughter around the Cabinet Table.

The rest of Europe had also changed. More and more countries had elected right-wing governments and adopted policies first implemented by GB Patriots, although change was a lot slower than in the UK. Nevertheless, the peoples of Europe once again felt comfortable within their own culture, which, as far as Michael was concerned, was something the Brussels' bureaucrats tried to destroy. But their constant meddling had backfired, as one by one, each country voted to leave the outdated institution. It would be another two years before the leader of Vlamms Belgan got his wish and turned the former EU Parliament Building into the Centre for European Arts and Culture, which naturally paid homage to the many and varied global cultures it had drawn upon, Africa and Asia in particular.

'Holding Back the Years' came floating through the sound system. Inside the marquee a spotlight picked out the happy couple as they held each other close and drifted round the dance floor.

Michael and Sadie had finally tied the knot. The ceremony was taking place in the grounds of Plumley Old Hall, their grand Cheshire residence. It was a private affair restricted to family and close friends. Having both been married before — it was Sadie's third time around the block — they wanted the least possible fuss; just a simple ceremony followed by a cosy meal. Besides, Michael didn't want to upset his many friends from the world of politics, show business and sport. So to avoid the tricky question of who to invite — which would have caused offence to anyone left out — he decided to keep it a secret until the after the event.

The night before the wedding Michael's son Richard and his wife Sophie travelled up from Bath. Richard was studying for a PhD in Advanced Chemical Engineering at the university, while Sophie ran her own veterinary practice. Richard was his only link with the past; both Haley and Emma refused to attend the wedding.

As soon as the couple arrived Michael took Richard for a walk in the grounds. He was eager for news about Haley.

"I've tried contacting her a dozen times over the past week, but she doesn't want to know," explained Richard. "Apparently I'm your lackey. Stupid cow. Mum reckons it's just a phase she's going through and that the best thing to do is leave her alone. Fine by me… Long phase though, don't you think?"

The sun was about to set, a fiery red sky streaked with black clouds: tomorrow promised to be a glorious day. "It's not a phase," said Michael, deeply wounded by his daughter's bloody-mindedness. "That's just wishful thinking on the part of your mother. To be honest Richard I'm really worried about her."

The old sibling rivalry flared up. "As if you

haven't got enough on your plate trying to run the country, you have to worry about her!" He had always known Haley was his dad's favourite from an early age — so was eager to stick the knife in. And just to show Michael he was aware of that favoritism, he added, "Always was a spoilt bitch."

"Don't talk about your sister like that." Michael looked wounded. His mind returned to the article in the *Guardian*. "You had a happy childhood, didn't you, Richard? I mean, you don't think I'm a narcissist?"

"Of course not Dad. If anyone's a narcissist it's Haley… You're worried about her, aren't you? I can tell. I am, to be honest. I wonder what she's up to?"

"I know exactly what she's up to: the security services are keeping an eye on her… This way."

They took a path that skirted the woods. He sighed. "The *last* thing I want is to spy on my own daughter, but she's left me no choice; the group she's involved with are lunatics. *Lunatics!* Especially that loser she's shacked up with."

"Oh yeah!" scoffed Richard. "Comrade Lonny. Mum's met him, you know."

"I know."

"Blimey. You really *are* monitoring her."

"I *have* to: national security."

Richard noticed the pained expression on his father's face. He needed to change the subject, and fast.

"Cheer up. You're getting married tomorrow."

"You're right. Time we headed back. You and

Sophie must be hungry."

They set off towards the house, a stunning Jacobean mansion silhouetted against the evening sky. Richard chuckled. "I bet you have to pinch yourself, don't you? Prime Minister: about to marry the woman of your dreams; house in the country. Not bad for a kid from Levenshulme."

Michael glowed from within. He winked at his son. "Not just a pretty face."

"Tell me about it. Half the women at Uni fancy you — lecturers *and* students. I can't tell you the amount of offers I've had once they find out I'm your son. Absolute stunners some of them. I tell you Dad, if I wasn't married I'd be in there like a—"

"*STOP!!!*"

A hooded figure carrying a gun suddenly emerged from the woods. Three armed Special Service officers followed, barking out orders.

Michael had been warned something like this might happen; according to the head of MI5, her operatives had picked up what she described as a 'seething undercurrent of discontent'. It was only a matter of time before…

A shot rang out.

The figure fell to the ground screaming in agony.

Richard couldn't believe what was happening; one minute he and his father were strolling along having a quiet chat, the next…

"We got him, sir," said one of the officers.

Michael set off towards the figure writhing

around in the grass.

"Sir! STOP! He's still armed!"

Michael ignored the officer and carried on walking, eager to find out who this person was.

"SIR! PLEASE!"

"*STOP DAD!*"

Before the officers took another step Michael had reached the figure. He knelt down and pulled off the hoddie — in his minds eyes he saw Haley staring up at him.

"It's alright officer. He's a she." He picked up a black object off the ground and held it up. "And she's armed alright… with a camera." Michael looked at the photographer. "Are you alright."

"No! I've been shot in the leg. I'm in fucking agony… *Ahhh*!"

"You'll live."

When the security officers ran over, Michael stood up. "You'd better call an ambulance."

"You should have seen Richard's face! Frightened wasn't the word. He wouldn't be much use as a bodyguard."

Sophie burst out laughing. All three were sitting in the dining room of Plumley Old Hall tucking in to roast venison.

"Alright Dad. Give me a break. How did I know she was *Paparazzi.*"

"They're obviously here for the wedding," said Sophie, helping herself to another portion of broccoli.

"Richard looked puzzled. "Beats me how she knew. I thought you said it was a secret."

Michael sighed. "It *is*… was. The security officer told me the photographer is freelance, and that she was acting alone. That means someone tipped her off. Those magazines pay a lot of money for exclusives."

"It *has* to be someone close to you or Sadie," mused Richard. Someone who knows about the wedding."

"Definitely no one from Sadie's side. They're all rolling in it."

"Who then?"

Michael picked up his wine glass. "I'll give you three guesses. She lives with a loser and would do anything to spoil the wedding."

Cheers rang out inside the marquee as Michael and Sadie left the dance floor and took their seats at the top table. To Sadie's left, David and her mother Caroline. To Michael's right, Richard and Sophie.

Caroline nudged Sadie's arm. "You look gorgeous, darling." She moved closer, whispering. "Make this the last time, eh?"

"Don't worry, Mummy. Let's face it, I'm not getting any younger."

Both women gave each other knowing smiles.

'Celebrate' by Kool and the Gang blasted through the speakers. There was a whoop as the rest of the guests rose from their tables and took to the dance floor. Michael was chatting with Sophie when he noticed a security officer enter the marquee and marched over.

What now?

The officer stood behind Michael and spoke in a calm but firm voice. "You need to come with me, Prime Minister."

Michael could tell by his expression that it had nothing to do with a rogue *Paparazzi.*

He kissed Sadie on the cheek. "Something's come up." He turned and followed the officer out of the marquee. It was a beautiful star-filled evening.

"What is it?"

"A bomb's gone off at the Royal Albert Hall, sir. It's carnage."

Shocked, he stared at the officer. Then it dawned on him. "It's The Last Night of The Proms!"

"Yes sir."

"Oh God... Anyone claimed responsibility?"

"No sir. Not yet."

"I need to get to London. Now!"

"It's all been taken care of."

Out of the darkness came the approaching sound of a helicopter. Moments later a blur of flashing lights and whirring rotor blades appeared above the house. A spotlight light lit up the back lawn as the helicopter picked out a space to land, slowly easing itself down.

Michael had to shout above the din. "Tell my wife I'll phone her later."

"Yes sir."

He hurried over and got in. It took off immediately. He watched from a side window as the marquee gradually got smaller and smaller. Suddenly the helicopter banked to the right and headed south.

On the way to London he spoke with the Home Secretary Grace Magars. The atrocity had only just occurred, she said, so details were a little sketchy. Apparently midway through the final rendition of 'Land of Hope and Glory' there was a huge explosion.

"The bomb was placed beneath the stage and ripped through the auditorium. Hundreds have been killed, Michael. Innocent concert-goers enjoying a night out." Her voice faltered. "It's terrible... Terrible."

"Calm down, Grace." There was a steely determination in his voice. "Whoever did this are going to wish they'd never been born."

As the helicopter approached the capital Michael sat glued to his smartphone watching the live news feed. It was a sickening sight. The world-famous concert hall was ringed with emergency vehicles — fire engines, ambulances. Smoked billowed from windows and doors. Soot-blackened people came staggering out screaming, their smart evening clothes torn to shreds. One unfortunate woman was slumped against the wall. A news crew ran over to her. Her face was badly burnt.

Sobbing hysterically she looked into the camera wild-eyed. "Why?... Why?"

Michael knew why. It was no coincidence the bomb went off in the middle of 'Land of Hope and Glory'. Whoever did this was sending him a message — with the general election less than a year away they were trying to destabalise the country and destroy everything he'd built. *Islamic extremists. Has to be! Or some left-wing radicals! I've been far too soft with these people. Not anymore!*

When he got to 10 Downing Street he dashed straight into a COBRA meeting. Senior ministers, security officials, and heads of the Intelligence Services were already gathered round the table, tense expressions on their faces.

Michael sat down and came straight to the point. "Any idea who did this?"

The head of MI5, Veronica Mayland, shook her head. "Not yet, Prime Minister."

"What!? No idea at all?""No, Prime Minister. We're still looking into it."

Michael was livid. "Looking into it! What do you people *do* all day?! I want whoever's responsible caught as soon as possible, do you understand?"

"It's not that simple, Pri—"

Michael smashed the table with his fist. "I've spent millions of pounds bringing your department up to date! So you better fucking well do it, or I'll find someone who can!"

"Yes, Prime Minister."

It was the first time anyone had heard Michael swear during an official meeting.

"And how the hell did someone managed to get a bomb into the Royal Albert Hall!?"

Veronica stared the table.

"You won't find the answer there! This was on your watch, Veronica, and I'm holding you personally responsible!! If I find out your department has missed anything, anything at all, I'll send you to prison! I mean it. Gone are the days when you people simply retire on a fat pension. Everyone's accountable in my administration." He glared at each person sitting round the table. "And I mean *everyone!*"

Grace Magars had never seen Michael so angry. He was losing his temper more and more these days, even with his most loyal ministers. For instance, when he was informed that the inflation rate had risen, he immediately summoned the Chancellor of the Exchequer and hauled him over the coals, accusing him of taking his eye off the ball.

Obviously the pressure he was under was enormous — the upcoming general election, the behavior of his errant daughter, the growing voices of dissent coming from all sections of the media, the increase in demonstrations. She knew how much he valued his reputation as a political icon and cultural trailblazer (his biography *A New Vision* had been translated into 27 languages, selling millions of copies worldwide). Grace was only too aware of the embarrassment Haley was causing; it was her department's job to monitor her after all. Only last week she reluctantly told him that Haley and her partner Lonny Katz had attended a meeting at the home of a well-known anarchist. Other prominent radicals were there, including the head of REBEL5, a shadowy anti-fascist group dedicated to overthrowing the establishment by violent means. After she'd finished telling him the details, Grace noticed the frozen look of anger on his face; he was staring into the distance, his eyes blazing.

As the COBRA meeting progressed Michael started drumming his fingers on the table. All he could hear from his so called 'experts' and 'trusted advisors' was waffle. None of them had the slightest idea about what to do or how to proceed. In the end his patience snapped. Tough decisive action was called for. Leadership, in other words!

First he addressed Veronica Mayland. "I want you to increase the monitoring of individuals and groups we consider enemies of the State. I don't care how you do it — phone intercepts, wire taps, hacks… anything that will give us the heads-up as to what's going on out there. If this had been done correctly in the first place we might have prevented tonight's bombing."

Desperate to improve her standing with the prime minister, nevertheless she was duty-bound to inform him of the privacy laws. "Obviously I'll have to apply to the courts for permission before—"

More obfuscation! "Just do it, for fuck's sake! Let me deal with the courts! This is a national emergency!"

"Y… yes, Prime Minister."

He glared at her. "Well? What are you waiting for?!"

Veronica shot out of her chair. "Certainly, Prime Minister." She gathered up her papers and hurried from the room.

Then he addressed Grace Magars.

"I want you to draw up a list of all known trouble-causers — Anarchists, Islamists, Marxists, political agitators — anyone involved in anti-government rhetoric deemed to incite violence. I want them arrested and interned for detailed questioning. Put them in the former migrant centers built by the last government. We'll finally get some proper use out of them."

XXII

"MICHAEL HOW *COULD* you? Your own daughter! Locked away like some terrorist!"

"She's not 'locked away'. She's being detained."

"Same *bloody* thing!.. For how long?"

"Depends what the security services find. Or how cooperative she is."

"She's been in there six weeks already!"

"These things take time, Emma. They have to be thorough."

"Heartless bastard."

"You saw what happened at the Albert Hall! Innocent people were murdered. I will not stand by and let that happen again."

It was a month before the general election and Michael was speaking to his ex-wife from the back of his official limousine. He was on his way to Highcliff Park in Gloucestershire, a twenty-eight-thousand acre estate, and one of the few stately homes still in private hands. He'd been taking calls all morning from his press secretary, Madeleine Stewart — apparently sections of the media were raging over the amount of arrests going on up and down the country, accusing the prime minister of running a police state.

After waiting for over an hour his ex-wife was finally put through.

"Haley had nothing to do with it! She may be a lot of things, Michael, but she's not a murderer."

"Don't you understand!? She's a member of a group who's openly calling for violent revolution. They could have planted that bomb for all we know."

"Ridiculous!"

"She's the leader's *girlfriend*, for heaven's sake! Imagine what the press would have said if she *hadn't* been arrested."

"Lonny's not a terrorist. He's a nice man."

Michael almost let slip he'd heard a recoding made by M15 of Lonny discussing armed insurrection with the leader of REBEL5. Most alarmingly of all, Haley was involved in the discussion, egging them on.

"Yes," he scoffed. "Richard told me you'd met him…" *Nice man*? You don't know the half of it. He's a dangerous individual who's dragging our daughter down with him… of her own accord by the way."

"Well I intend to hire the best lawyer possible, even if I go to bankrupt in the process."

"And you're well within your rights to do so."

Emma gasped. "My God. *Listen* to you. How cold you've become Michael. This is our daughter we're talking about."

"No one is above the law, including our daughter."

"Oh go to hell!"

The line went dead. Michael sighed. He stared out of the window at the shifting Gloucestershire countryside — dry stone walls, wheat fields, farmhouses, country pubs.

His few moments of peace were interrupted by a call from Sadie complaining about the architect she'd hired to design and build a summer house in the grounds of their Cheshire home. "I keep telling him I want it by the lake, but he says the ground is too boggy."

"He must know what he's talking about, Em'. He's an archi—"

"He's a complete idiot! I can't cope with him anymore. You'll have to sort him out... When are you coming home?"

"I'll be back at Number 10 around midnight."

"Midnight!"

"I have a speech to make at—"

"Forget it. I'll do it myself."

Next on the line was Madeleine Stewart. It was good news for once.

"The opinion polls have just been released. The country is right behind you on this, despite the battering you're taking in the press. We're on course for another huge majority."

He was elated. "You can always trust the common-sense of the British people. They seem to have an inbuilt antenna for this sort of thing."

"Thought you'd be pleased... Are you at Highcliff Park yet?"

"Just pulling in through the gates."

"The Downing Street photographer is already there ... Remember, your left side is your best side."

"Thanks Madeleine. Talk later."

After driving a mile or so through a picturesque landscape of rolling parkland the house came into view. Highcliff Park was more like a palace than a stately home; a spectacular neoclassical mansion surrounded by manicured gardens. A huge marble fountain could be seen fronting the house. At its centre was a colossal bronze statue of Neptune, a jet of water spurting high into the air from a conch shell balanced on his right shoulder. As the water reached its apex and cascaded down, it glinted rainbow-like in the sun.

Michael was here because of an invitation he'd received from Lord Francome. He had just come off the phone with the head of NATO concerning Russia's build-up of tanks and artillery on the Finnish border when he was handed the letter. As soon as he saw the name and family crest Michael's pulse rate shot up; this was the man whose ancestors had once owned the sugar plantation that had enslaved Bartholomew Francome Taylor, and had more than likely worked to death many of his family.

His lordship was keen to meet the prime minister, the letter said. Perhaps he would like to pop over for lunch one day? Michael knew why. Over breakfast a few days before, he'd read an article in the *Sunday Times* about the Francome family's involvement in the slave trade; the vast amount of wealth created through their various sugarcane plantations across the Caribbean. And according to the *Sunday Times* they'd managed to hang on to that wealth — they were one of the richest families in England. The reporter had dug deeper, uncovering the fact that Michael's ancestor had once 'belonged' to the Francomes. It was obviously because of this, and the ensuing publicity, that the present Lord Francome had reached out to him. Make peace with the past, so to speak. Michael thought long and hard about whether or not to accept the invitation. He was wary of opening a can of worms. Besides, as he often told the media when asked about his ancestors, "Raking over old wounds never did anyone any good. We have to look to the future."

But there were one or two questions still unresolved, questions that haunted him. Michael knew a lot about Bartholomew *after* he'd left Jamaica, but nothing about his life on the island. More importantly, he was keen to go back further, to find out which Africa country he originated from. Maybe the final piece of jigsaw lay in the Francome family archives? After much deliberation he decided to accept.

Michael stepped from the limousine and stared at the house, its magnificent dome, its grandiose stone portico and endless rows of sash windows. Behind him he could hear the plashing of the fountain. There was a sense of timelessness about the place, a sense of melancholy, a feeling of being sealed off from the world.

It was Lord Francome himself who emerged

through the polished front door and sauntered down the steps to greet him. A tall stout man in his early sixties with a chubby face, thick sensual lips and thinning blonde hair, he was dressed casually in light grey slacks and an open-neck white shirt.

"Prime Minister! Welcome to Highcliff Park. Delighted you could make it."

The Downing Street photographer circled them as they approached one another. The moment they shook hands past and present collided in a blinding flash. Michael felt a bolt of electricity shoot up his arm; this was the hand that had raped, bullied, whipped and murdered an entire people.

He steadied himself. "Thank you for inviting me, Lord Francome." He gazed at the house. "You have a beautiful home."

"Thank you. Yes. Upkeep costs a fortune I'm afraid… If you'd like to step this way?"

He followed Lord Francome up the steps and into the entrance hall. Michael remembered his visit to Sadie's house in Mottram St. Andrew all those years ago; how overwhelmed he'd felt when first walking in. Highcliff Park, well, this was something else. The room was based on a Roman basilica. It was filled with Doric columns and featured classical Roman statues and gilded trophy panels. Set in niches between each column were marble busts of ancient Greek philosophers — Socrates, Plato, Aristotle — suggesting the Francomes were natural heirs of the two great civilizations.

"The house was built by Robert Adam," remarked Lord Francome, matter-of-fact. "Apparently this particular room was inspired by the *Villa Madama* in Rome… This way. I do hope you're hungry"

Next they headed down the Long Gallery. Evenly spaced between exquisite Chinese lacquered cabinets inlaid with mother-of-pearl were magnificent portraits of the Francome family, generations of them. Halfway along the carpeted gallery Lord Francome stopped opposite a full-length portrait of a chubby-faced young man with a peaches and cream complexion wearing a red velvet cloak trimmed with ermine. What was different from the other portraits was that he was standing in a tropical landscape. To his left was a large plantation house, while directly behind him, acres and acres of sugarcane fields stretched toward the horizon. Standing next to the man, staring up at him with absolute devotion, was a young slave boy wearing ragged striped shorts holding a fan made of ostrich feathers. Michael recongised the painting from the *Sunday Times* article. Seeing it this close he was moved beyond words.

Lord Francome coughed nervously. "This is err, this is the fourth earl. He was painted by Sir Thomas Lawrence in 1825 to celebrate his ennoblement in the House of Lords." To alleviate his embarrassment he made a little joke. "Of course that was before your government abolished it. I do miss the restaurant there. The shepherd's pie was superb. Have you ever—"

Michael took a step towards the painting. Up-close it revealed even more detail. What caught his eye was the background; the vast of acreage of sugarcane. In the *Sunday Times* photograph the fields were covered in black dots. As Michael leaned in he could see that these dots were in fact people; hundreds of naked black men, women and children toiling under a scorching Caribbean sun. He stood there in silence. The photographer crouched down and took a couple of shots.

"Lunch is served, your Lordship."

Michael blinked. He turned to see the butler standing at the end of the Long Gallery.

"Thank you, Alan. We're just coming… Prime Minister?" Lord Francome gestured at the butler. "Shall we?"

"Oh yes! Sorry."

They walked towards the open door at the far end.

"Yes, I often look at that painting," continued his lordship. "Dreadful what took place back then. Absolutely dreadful. My daughter keeps banging on at me to take the damned thing down. But as I never tire of telling her, hiding it away won't change a thing. None of us can escape our past. We're lumbered with it, whether we like or not. The good as well as the bad. The important thing is, we have to acknowledge it and move on, which is why I invited you here today."

"Couldn't have put it better myself."

"Tell me, do you like roast pheasant?"

"Yes, very much."

"Excellent."

Before they entered the dining room Michael told the photographer to take a break. "I'll call you when I need you, Ailsa."

"Yes sir."

"Ask the housekeeper for some tea," suggested Lord Francome.

Ailsa nodded and walked back up the Long Gallery.

The table seated twenty, though only three places were set. Unlike the rest of the house the dining room was paneled throughout in dark oak, giving it the feel of an Edwardian gentleman's club. The walls were hung with oil paintings by Constable, Palmer, and Banks, depicting bucolic views of the English countryside.

"The work of the sixth Earl," remarked Lord Francome, noticing the confused look on Michael's face as they made their way to the table. "Room sticks out like a sore thumb doesn't it? Apparently he wanted to bring the house up to date. Lord knows why... Won't you sit down, Prime Minister... Luckily he died in his twenties before he could do anymore damage. Blew his brains out over some woman... Was it ever thus?" He smiled as he took his seat at the head of the table. "Bit of a black sheep the sixth Earl. Every family's got one."

"You can say that again," said Michael,

comparing his elegant surroundings to the detention centre where Haley was currently residing. He wondered if she was eating properly — she'd always been a fussy eater — and if the kitchen was aware of her food allergies (as soon as she was arrested Michael had telephoned the governor personally to inform him of her dietary needs). His own daughter, an 'undesirable element.' However did it come to this?

Lord Francome was quick to pick up on his guest's sad expression. "Yes, I've read about your daughter. If it's any consolation Prime Minister, I have a rebel of my own." Footsteps could be heard walking up the Long Gallery. "Speaking of which... My youngest daughter, Juliana. She insisted on joining us. Hope you don't mind?"

"Of course not."

Lord Francome raised his eyes flirtatiously. "She's a huge fan of yours."

The moment she stepped into the room Michael lost all sense of perspective: Haley, Nato, the general election, the nationwide riots, the rise in inflation, the worrying developments in the Middle East, everything faded into the background. It was just him, sitting there, looking at her.

Juliana was nineteen-years-old and wore a dizzyingly short micro-skirt and tight red top; her fragile, stick-thin figure, chopped blonde hair and huge blue eyes giving her the look of a 1960's model. There was a willfulness about her that bordered on arrogance; a blue-blooded, aristocratic version of Sadie supercharged for the 21st century.

She walked to her father and threw her arms around him, kissing him on the lips.

"Hi Daddy."

"Hello, Ju-Ju."

Resting her head on her father's shoulder she looked at Michael and smiled. "Hello Michael."

She spoke with a lazy, penetrating drawl, her full lips giving her an alluring sexual pout. Michael glanced at her father, and then remembered the faces of the other Francomes in the Long Gallery.

Obviously runs in the family.

"Where are your manners Juliana. Address him as Prime Minister."

Michael laughed, "That's alright, Lord Francome. Everyone calls me Michael."

"See, Daddy. Michael doesn't give a shit."

"Juliana! *Please!*.. I do apologise. You wouldn't think my daughter has been educated at the best schools. And I stress the word 'schools'. She never lasted long at any of them." Despite the apparent scolding there was a look of pride on Lord Francome's face.

She sat down opposite Michael.

Most women were star-struck when meeting him for the first time, staring at him with a kind of religious devotion. Juliana's look was something he'd never encountered before; she had an innocent yet challenging expression, as if daring him to do something. Unnerved, he looked away. When he looked back she was grinning.

He fumbled with his napkin and said the first thing that came into his head. "Ju-Ju? Erm… where did that come from, Lord Francome?"

"When my daughter was born, my sister's four-year-old son couldn't say Juliana. He kept calling her Ju-Ju, so the name stuck."

"Cute."

Juliana sniggered.

There was a polite tap on the door.

"Come."

The butler appeared, pushing a trolley.

"What are we having Daddy?"

"Roast pheasant."

"Yummy!"

When the meal was set out and Michael picked up his knife and fork, both father and daughter closed their eyes and bowed their heads. He quickly did the same

"Thank you for this food, Lord. And bless those gathered around this table."

"Amen."

"Amen," added Michael.

Juliana opened her eyes and picked up her cutlery. "I'm famished!"

During the meal Lord Francome asked Michael how the investigation into the Royal Albert Hall terrorist attack was going. "I was supposed to be there that night you know, but was ill with Covid."

"Really?"

"Umm. Terrible business... I had it for over two weeks."

"We're still looking into it. Rest assured we'll find the perpetrators and hang every last one of them."

"Hear! Hear! Best thing you ever did, reinstating capital punishm—"

"You're here because of that painting, aren't you?" said Juliana, interrupting her father. "Because of that article in the *Sunday Times?*"

"Yes, I suppose so."

"Has my father apolgised?"

"No. And he doesn't have to."

"Why not? If someone had kidnapped my family and worked them to death I'd want more than an apology. I'd kill the bastard."

Again Lord Francome was amused, a faint smile appearing around his eyes. "Bugger for holding grudges my daughter." He picked up his wine glass and held it up to the light. "Hate to get on the wrong side of her." He took a sip. "What do you think of the wine, Prime Minister? My grandfather laid it down in nineteen—"

"Violence never solved anything," now it was Michael's turn to interrupt his lordship, "it only makes things worse."

"Who cares, if it solves the problem?"

Michael had do stop himself from smiling. Her willfulness fascinated him.

"God help this country if Juliana was ever in

charge," said Lord Francome. "There'd be nuclear war in less than a week."

"I'm not *that* bad Daddy!"

"Really!? Well we'll soon see what happens to this estate when I'm gone." He turned to Michael. "I don't have a son, so everything goes to Juliana."

"Lucky girl." Michael took a sip of wine and glanced at Juliana. "That's a lot of responsibility. How d'you think you'll cope?"

"No idea." She grinned cheekily. "Pay me a visit and find out."

"I might just do that." The words came out before he knew it. He stared to blush.

Desperate to cover his tracks he glanced at Lord Francome. "Hopefully it won't be for a long time yet."

But it was too late; father and daughter were smirking at one another.

Midway through dessert Juliana's phone pinged. She looked at the screen. "Shit!" She stood up. "Sorry, I have to go." She kissed her father and hurried out of the room, ignoring Michael completely.

Lord Francome shook his head. "That girl's a complete mystery to me. Just like her mother." He drifted into the past for a moment before looking at Michael. "My fourth wife…Died from a heroin overdose when Juliana was five years old." He regained his composure. "Still, no use crying over spilt milk."

Michael took advantage of his host's reflective

mood to address the reason for his visit. "As I said in my reply to your invitation, I'd love to see the archives from the Francome sugarcane estate in Jamaica."

"Ah yes! The archives."

"You do have them?"

"Of course! They're set out in the library." He noticed Michael was fingering his napkin impatiently. "No rush. We'll have coffee first… You're the fourth prime minister to visit Highcliff Park you know."

"Oh yes?"

"Yes. The last one was Margaret Thatcher… Dreadful woman."

As promised, the archives pertaining to the Francomes' Jamaican sugarcane estates were laid out on a large walnut table — four leather-bound volumes going back to the start of the slave trade, dated and stamped with the name of each plantation; charming names like 'Windy Hill' and 'Golden Valley.'

"The Francomes had *four* plantations!?" asked Michael, surprised.

"That was just in Jamaica. We had twenty-three in all, spread right across the Caribbean." There was a hint of pride in his lordship's voice."

Twenty-three!

Michael's head was spinning as he tried to imagine how many slaves the Francomes must have owned. *Thousands! Across the centuries tens of thousands!*

"Your ancestor came to Britain in 1838 you say?" asked his Lordship.

"That's right; the same year slavery was abolished in the Caribbean. According to Bartholomew's marriage certificate, he was twenty when he got married. That was in 1839. That would make him nineteen when he left the island."

Michael noticed Lord Francome stare off into space.

"Anything the matter?"

"I was just thinking… when you hear details like that it really brings home to one that these people — people my family treated as mere chattels — were living, breathing individuals with hopes and dreams." He shook his head. "Terrible. Absolutely terrible."

Michael felt his eyes moisten. "Beautifully put, Lord Francome."

The two men stood in silence, the only sound the ticking of a French ormolu clock on the mantelpiece. Michael's gaze drifted through the window and out across the estate. He then glanced around the beautifully decorated library with its Chippendale furniture and wonderfully carved Renaissance bronzes. A feeling of nausea swept over him.

Lord Francome picked up one of the ledgers. "Right. You look in this one: Windy Hill. I'll look in Golden Valley. If we can't find Bartholomew's name we'll try the other two volumes: Sugarland and Kingston Farm."

Before they sat down Lord Francome rang for

the butler and told him to serve tea at 4 p.m. They each drew up a chair and began pouring over their respective ledgers.

Michael went through each page meticulously. The names of the slaves — all anglicised and with the prefix 'Francome' — were written in beautifully slanted copperplate, along with their age, sex, tribe, and country of origin — *'Francome, John. Male. 22. Akan. Gold Coast."*

Michael noticed that nearly all the slaves were captured Akan people. He took out his phone and Googled 'Akan.'

'The Akan people are a Kwa group living primarily in present-day Ghana. The Akan speak dialects within the Central Tano branch of the Potou—Tano subfamily of the Niger—Congo family. Subgroups of the Akan people include: the Agona, Akuapem, Akwamu, Akyem, Anyi, Ashanti, Baoulé, Bono, Chakosi, Fante, among others. The Akan subgroups all have cultural attributes in common; most notably the tracing of matrilineal descent in the inheritance of property, and for succession to high political office.'

High political office!

Michael was stunned.

"Did you find him, Prime Minister?" asked Lord Francome, noticing Michael's expression.

"Err, no. Not yet." He cast his eye down the page and shook his head. "So many people."

"Yes. Shocking isn't it" The ormolu clock chimed 4 p.m. "Ah! Here's Alan with the tea... Oh excellent! He's brought cake! Oh well done Alan!"

The butler pushed the trolley to the table. "Anything else your Lordship?"

"Not for the moment. Thank you."

When the butler had left the room Lord Francome picked up the antique Meissen teapot. Vividly painted in rich colours, it depicted a classical hunting scene of horses, riders and hounds chasing a fox across an English meadow.

"I'll be Mother… Milk? Sugar?"

"White please. No sugar."

Lord Francome poured the tea through a Georgian silver tea strainer into two Meissen cups. He cut himself a thick slice of sponge cake and put it on a matching side plate. "Do help yourself." He picked up his cup and saucer and carried them over to the settee by the fireplace. He sat down, gave his tea a quick stir then took a bite of cake. "*Umm!* Delicious." He glanced over at Michael who was still looking at the ledger. "Tea's going cold. Nothing worse than cold—"

"Found him! Oh my God!"

"Really? Oh well done. Which plantation?... Prime Minister?"

Michael grabbed his phone and took a photo of the page. He was elated. Unable to keep still he began to pace up and down. "Finally. *Finally!*" He walked over to the settee and sat down.

"You've forgotten your tea, Prime—."

"Kingston Farm! He lived on the Kingston Farm… In St. Ann's Bay."

"St. Ann's Bay? Really? We still have a house there... Well I never."

"What?! You have a house in St. Ann's Bay? On the actual sugarcane estate?"

"The Francomes don't own the land anymore, but yes. It was formerly the plantation manager's house; the one in the painting of the fourth Earl you saw earlier. I go there twice a year. Get away from our dreadful weather. Absolute godsend."

Lord Francome saw how excited Michael was. He suddenly had an idea. "Would you like to go, Prime Minister?"

"Go?"

"To the house in St. Ann's Bay. Absolute peach of a place."

"Really!?"

"Of course! We could go together if you like? I could show you around."

Michael's heart pounded. "Show me around! You'd do that?"

"Of course. It would be my pleasure."

"Yes! Yes! I'd love to, Lord Francome!" Present day came crashing in. "After the election, if that's possible?"

"Right you are then! After the election it is!"

XXIII

THE CELL DOOR OPENED. Haley trudged in and flopped down onto her bunk. The guard closed the door, locking it from the outside with a jangling of keys.

"Well?" Her cellmate Bev stuck her head over the top bunk. "Say anything?"

"Nothing *to* say."

"What about Lonny? Have you—"

Haley put her index finger to her lips and shook her head. Bev kept forgetting the cell was probably bugged. Oh shit! Of course! She nodded her head to say she understood.

"Have you eaten yet?"

Haley smiled. "Not yet… God knows why they keep questioning me. I've told them a thousand times Lonny and I had nothing to do with it. We're against violence of any sort." She raised her eyes and grinned as if to say. 'As if!'

Bev played along. "That's what I keep telling 'em."

"Six weeks I've been in this place. Six *fucking* weeks!" Haley imagined the fascist scumbag listening in at GCHQ or whatever government rat hole they were based at, so shouted, "WHAT'S HAPPENED TO INNOCENT UNTIL PROVEN GUILTY, YOU FUCKERS!"

"Yeah! Fascist pigs!"

Bev was a thirty-year-old social worker from Leeds. She'd been arrested while taking part in a civil rights rally outside the Home Office. She was new to this type of thing. Politics used to bore her, but she'd become interested after one of her neighbours — "A really nice Hungarian woman who's lived here for years" — was deported for not having the correct paperwork. "Pissed me off that did." The following week she joined a civil liberties group based in Leeds city centre. It wasn't long before she was out on demonstrations. "Cunt that Prime Minister."

She knew Haley was Michael Taylor's daughter, so had kept her opinions to herself until she heard Haley badmouth him. After that she let rip, with Haley's blessing. But only in the exercise yard, and only with her hand covering her mouth (it was rumored the government had brought in lip-readers to spy on them with binoculars during their daily exercise). That was the way things were these days. Fascist Britain or what!

"Had some good news, though," said Haley. "Mum's hired Michael Maidstone. You know; that shit-hot human-rights lawyer."

Bev swung her legs over the side and jumped down off the top bunk. "Hey! I've heard of him! He's the one who got that journalist off those sedition charges."

Haley sat up. "That's him. Costs an absolute fortune. Hope he can do the same for me and Lonny." She saw a look of disappointment sweep across Bev's face. Haley suddenly felt guilty — she was no different from anyone else in there, so why should she get preferential treatment just because her mother had money.

Money again! Fucking money!!

"D'you know what, Bev? Fuck the lawyer. I'm staying in here with the rest of you."

It was only after lights-out that the two women felt free to talk, and then only in a whisper. Anyway what did it matter; even if the security services *did* hear them, Haley doubted they'd be interested in women's shit.

Later that night, with the cell in pitch darkness, Bev asked, "Where did you meet Lonny?"

"At his bookshop in Hoxton."

"Was it love at first sight?"

"Not really. He grew on me."

"I've known a few guys like that. They're the dangerous ones."

"Tell me about it."

"What was it you liked about him?"

"He was the first man I ever met who didn't want to wrap me in cotton wool."

"He treats you like shit, you mean?"

"*No* Bev. He doesn't treat me like shit. No way would I put up with that. He treats me as an equal. He respects my views and doesn't talk down to me; unlike some men I've known." She thought about her father, the way he used to laugh at her when she was a teenager whenever she spoke about politics.

Once, when the family was sitting at the dinner table — she must have been what, sixteen? — he went ballistic after she told him she'd joined No Borders, explaining, "we believe in freedom of movement for all, and want the barriers imposed on us by capitalist elites and their governments to be dismantled."

Michael had hit the roof. "You don't know what you're talking about! Those 'capitalist elites' are the reason you're sitting in a million pound house. So keep your mouth shut in future."

He'd never spoken to her like that. Ever. To show her disgust Emma got up from the table and left the room.

Still her father hadn't finished. "Look what you've done … upsetting your mother like that."

She was about to fire back that *he* was the one who'd upset *her*, when Richard nudged her foot under the table. Born peacemaker that boy.

A month later Haley was released. It was the day after the general election. The guard escorting her to the gate took great delight in telling her, "Your dad's in charge for another five years." He gave a fist pump. "Get in!"

Dismayed, she shot back, "Don't be so sure."

She asked if Lonny was being released. No. He was still being questioned. She wondered if it was some kind of sick joke on her father's part, letting her out on the day he was back in power. Show her who's boss, knowing him. The only silver lining was that the government's majority had been significantly reduced.

Her mother was there to meet her. Emma had driven up to London the previous night had and stayed in a hotel close to the detention centre. As soon as she saw Haley emerged through the high-security gates she jumped out of the car and rushed towards her, hugging her tightly.

"Oh darling! Darling!"

"Alright, Mum. Calm down,"

"Sorry, I'm… I'm so relieved you're out." She stood back and looked at her tatty jeans, red Doc Martens and black donkey jacket. "You've lost weight!"

"So would you with the shit they serve in there."

"And those awful clothes."

"What's wrong with them?"

She let it drop. "Come on, let's get you home."

They walked towards her Range Rover.

"What about Lonny?"

"The bastards have kept him in."

Emma noticed how much her daughter had changed during her ten week incarceration; how angry she'd become. She seemed to have a permanent frown, and her bright blue eyes were loaded with hate.

They got in the car. Emma turned the key in the ignition. The *Today* programme came on the radio; the presenter was interviewing various guests about the election result.

"Turn that shit off!" said Haley. It was as though she'd been poked by a cattle prod, so vociferous was her reaction.

"Alright, darling. Calm down. We're—"

"*Don't* tell me to calm down Mum! *Please!* I've just spent ten fuckin' weeks inside!"

"I know. I'm sorry." She took hold of her daughter's hand. "You've been through a lot haven't you? Yes. To think your own father had—"

"Don't mention that Nazi to me *ever* again!"

Instead of driving into central London, as Haley expected, she kept seeing signs for the M1.

"Where are we going?"

"I'm taking you home."

"Home?"

"Wilmslow."

"*Wilmslow!* What the fuck do I want t go to Wilmslow for? I live in Hoxton."

"But I thought—"

"Just *do* it, Mum!"

Emma realised it was useless to argue, so she changed direction and headed into central London. Driving past The Royal Courts of Justice Haley looked at the building contemptuously. "'Justice'! There's no justice in this country anymore."

Further along Emma noticed Michael's old law chambers. Across the street was the pub where they first met. She stared at its Victorian façade. It only seemed like yesterday... she had been playing pool with a friend when a good-looking black guy approached and started chatting. When he told her he was training to become a barrister she was shocked.

"Really?! You don't seem the legal type."

"Why not?"

"I don't know. I've only just met you, but you seem more happy-go-luck—"

"*Mum!!!* Watch the road for fuck's sake! You nearly hit that bus!"

Emma burst out crying.

"Oh for God's sake take me home."

When they pulled up outside *Veritas* Emma was about to suggest they go for lunch somewhere nice but Haley opened the door and jumped out.

"Thanks Mum. See you soon, yeah."

She watched as Haley crossed the pavement and disappeared inside the bookshop. Its dusty windows and peeling front door made her heart sink. Distraught, she called her partner Ben at the house they shared in Wilmslow, the same house she and Michael had bought years ago.

"I've... I've lost her..." was all she could say, before leaning over the steering wheel and bursting into tears.

XXIV

Michael's official limousine left Buckingham Palace and drove down the Mall. Cheering crowds lined the route, though not as many as five years ago, which irked him somewhat. He had just met with King William. After a brief chat about their respective families the monarch invited him to form the next government. Before he left, the king mentioned the increasing number of riots taking place around the UK, and how worried he was. Michael explained that a small number of left-wing radicals were behind them, whipping things up, and that he was bringing in legislation to charge them with terror offences.

Turning into Whitehall his phone pinged. He looked at the screen — 'Unknown number'. It was a text. Intrigued, he opened it.

Hey! Congrats! Let's celebrate… Juliana.

The cheeky…

He pictured her sitting across the table at Highcliff Park, her willful, pixie face, her mascara-ringed her eyes, her sexy body. *How the hell you get this number, young lady?* Then he realised. *Of course! Daddy knows everyone.*

He ignored the message but somehow found himself on her Instagram page. There was Ju-Ju — Lady Juliana Constance Francome — surfing in Bali, ballooning in Kenya, partying in Marrakech, surrounded by equally beautiful boys and girls. He was drawn to one selfie in particular — almost naked in a lime-green, dental-floss bikini, Juliana was at some beach party in the Maldives; the sun was about to set and she was staring into the camera with the cutest of grins as if to say "Look everyone! Aren't I totally amazing!" He had to admit that, yes, she was.

Totally.

The final cabinet meeting before the Parliamentary summer recess was held the following morning. It was hardly the most ideal start to the day. After breakfast Sadie had flounced off to Paris after yet another argument about the summer house. Then the Governor of Bank of England phoned to say that due to an alarming rise in inflation, he was left with no alternative but to raise interest rates.

First topic on the agenda was how to deal with the increasing civil unrest since the general election. The Home Secretary suggested limiting the numbers of people allowed to demonstrate. Michael was scathing. "It's no good pussy-footing around. I want more surveillance. Better intel. As for the marches, we should ban them altogether. Go after the ring leaders." He was thinking of Lonny Kanz, who had just been released from detention due to lack of evidence. "Give them ten years hard labour. That'll stop… What's the matter?"

The members of the cabinet were glancing at one another sheepishly.

"What the hell's *wrong* with you?"

The Attorney General spoke up tentatively. "Won't that make things worse, Prime Minister? I mean, no government has ever gone that far. People have rights after all."

The rest of the Cabinet nodded their heads in agreement.

Michael smashed the table with his fist. "Rights? Rights? *That* lawless rabble? They've got no 'rights' whatsoever! Now listen to me the lot of you. The country has given us a mandate. Our citizens expect us to keep the peace. They have 'rights' too, don't forget. If we don't act, and act decisively, it'll make us look weak, and the demonstrations will only get worse. Before you know it…" His phoned pinged. Sadie? He glanced at the screen. — 'Unknown number', "… Before you know it, they'll be anarchy. *Anarchy!* So show some backbone. We're GB Patriots for heaven's sake, not the fucking Conservatives!"

Michael sprayed a generous amount of Creed Spice and Wood cologne onto his face. He loved the way, post shave, it gave his skin an electric tingle. Sadie had given it to him during a shopping trip to New York. She said that, according to the blurb, the fragrance was inspired by the legendary meeting between Cleopatra and Mark Anthony. Forbidden love; a story as old as time.

He stared at his refection in the mirror.

One drink. What harm can it do?

He'd replied to Juliana's text straight after the

fractious Cabinet meeting. Once again she suggested meeting for drinks. Why not? He needed cheering him up. And besides, Sadie was in Paris so it was the perfect opportunity. To cover himself, he texted back to say he would meet her at his private club in St. James to discuss the *Sunday Times* article; there were one or two questions he'd still like to ask.

Juliana grinned when she read that.

When he arrived at his club he was surprised to see her in the bar knocking back champagne cocktails. She was wearing a low cut, skin-tight black dress that made her appear even skinnier. Her blonde hair stood up in unruly tomboy tuffs and she wore a pair of scuffed, laceless tennis shoes.

As he approached she smiled and ordered two more champagne cocktails. When he got to the bar she leaned over and kissed him on the cheek. "Hi… Hey! Someone smells nice."

His face flushed. "How did you manage to get in? Women aren't allowed?"

"Daddy's a member. Anyway, my great grandfather formed the club shit knows how many years ago along with a couple of friends. He had it written into the constitution that female members of the Francome family were given lifelong membership." She stuck out her tongue. "So there!"

"I might have known," laughed Michael. "I've never seen your father in here?"

"No," she replied, vaguely, her mind elsewhere. Noticing his immaculately tailored black suit she suddenly perked up. "You look *really* handsome. Black suits you." She glanced at her dress and gave him a nudge."Twins!"

He looked at her milk-white skin. "Hardly!" Her breasts were tiny; two peaches floating below his eyeline. He imagined ripping off her dress and —

"We're eating here. Daddy says the restaurant's really good."

"Fine."

The barman was about to serve two champagne cocktails when Juliana stood up. "Take them to my table would you?"

"Yes, your ladyship." He glanced at Michael. "Good evening Prime Minister."

"Hello, Trevor. How's the family?"

"Fine, thank you, sir. The little one's just—"

"Come on! I'm starving!"

Michael followed her into the restaurant. "You have your own table? I'm impressed."

"My family do."

The Francome's table was set in an alcove in the far corner. Michael picked up the menu and glanced around the restaurant. It was half full. "I've always wondered whose table this was. I've never seen anyone sitting here."

"Daddy doesn't come up to town very often. He prefers Paris."

"Hang on… I *have* seen someone sitting here. It was a while back; an odd-looking man wearing a black leather jacket. He was with a Chinese boy."

Juliana smirked. "Oh yes. Uncle Francis… *Anyway*, how are you?"

"Exhausted. I've not been sleeping too well recently." Why the hell did he say that?

"You're not up for going dancing later then?"

He laughed. "Dancing! At my age?"

"You look OK to me." She leaned back in her chair, lowering her head to accentuate her big eyes. "Come *onnnn*. It'll be fun. You remember what fun is, don't you?" It was a look she had perfected as child to get her own way.

Michael smiled. "Oh I know what fun is, Juliana. Don't *you* worry."

She leaned forward. "I bet you do."

They held each other's gaze.

"Ready to order?" The waiter crashed the moment.

"Oh yes!" said Michael. "Hello, John. I'll err… I'll have the steak please."

"Yes sir. Well done as usual?"

"Well done."

"Yes sir. And what can I get you, Lady Francome?"

She glanced at the menu. "Let's see…"

Michael was mesmerised by her slender shoulders. He'd never seen such flawless white skin; catching the light it glowed with a pearly softness,

"… I'll have the lobster… And a bottle of Pomerol: the Saint Émellion"

"Yes, your ladyship."

Michael felt the need to change the subject.

"How *is* Lord Francome? He prefers Paris, you say?"

She nodded. "He's got an apartment there. As a matter of fact he's there now."

So was Sadie. Small world. "Wonderful city."

"I prefer Berlin."

The beautiful young Fräulein standing outside the Reichstag flashed into his mind; overcome with emotion she was smiling and crying. *Maybe I'm not too old to go dancing?* "No, I've got an early start tomorrow."

Juliana stared at him, confused.

Michael's face started to burn. "Sorry. Miles away." He coughed nervously and said, loud enough for the next table to hear. "Yes, it was good of Lord Francome to invite me to Highcliff Park. Reading the archives was a great help. Do thank him for me."

"That's why I'm here… Well, one of the reasons… He's going to Jamaica on Monday; to our house in St. Ann's Bay. He wants to know if you still want to come."

"Of course! That would be amazing."

When he got back to Number 10 there was a voice message on his private landline: Sadie. "You're out, as usual... I'm going to Provence to spend a few weeks with Fran and Maria. See you when I see you. Be good."

Michael erased the message. An empty feeling washed over him. About to turn in for the night his phone pinged. It was a text from Lord Francome —

Meet me in the first class lounge at Heathrow at 10am

on Monday.

Another text came through straight after.

Juliana — Loved tonight. Shame you had to leave early. x

XXV

Despite reassuring the head of MI5 that he didn't require his usual security team, she insisted otherwise. It was against protocol for a prime minister to travel without armed protection. It was set in stone. Sorry.

Michael was fed up of living in a goldfish bowl and wanted some privacy for once.

"But Lord Francome always hires his own security when he's on the island, so what's the point?"

In the end they agreed on a compromise — he would take his personal bodyguard Reg and his assistant Gavin, a former SAS solider.

"They're to stay in the background, is that understood? It's supposed to be a private holiday. I won't enjoy it if they're hanging around."

"Very well. They'll fly economy. You won't know they're there."

When he walked into the British Airways' First Class lounge spontaneous applause broke out. Although it happened wherever he went, it always gave him a kick. He smiled modestly, raising his hand in acknowledgement. An eight-year-old boy ran up and asked him for a selfie. He crouched down, put his arm around the boy's shoulder and they both smiled. Delighted, the boy ran back to his parents.

Michael glanced round the room but couldn't see Lord Francome. What he did see, on the wall above the bar, was a framed photo of himself alongside one of King Charles.

"Someone's popular."

Michael's jaw hit the floor. Juliana was sitting on a bar stool smirking.

"Surprise!"

His pulse took off. "Oh hi!" He made his way over. "Your father didn't mention you were coming… Neither did you."

"Thought I'd surprise you."

"You've certainly done that…Where is he, by the way?"

"Paris. He's not well."

"That's a shame," he lied. "Nothing serious I hope."

"Dicky heart. Runs in the family… So it's just you and me I'm afraid."

Michael couldn't believe his luck. "That's a shame."

Juliana was hurt. "Come on, it'll be fun."

"I'm joking! I'm joking!"

She slapped him on the arm. "I'll get you back for that."

"Oh God, your father warned me not to get on the wrong side of you."

"Be afraid. Be very afraid." Her smile returned and she motioned to her Bloody Mary. "Drink?"

"Bit early for me." He slid onto the bar stool and ordered a coffee.

Juliana raised her glass at the two photos above

the bar. "Cheers, your Majesty."

She nudged him in the ribs. "Guess which one's which."

"Cheeky!" Oh yes. This was going to be fun. He glanced at her ripped jeans, faded denim jacket and flip-flops. "Isn't there a dress code travelling first class?"

"There is, yeah."

He thought back to his club in St. James'. "But not for you."

"Not for me."

"Don't tell me; your father owns British Airways?"

"Of *course* not, silly! He *is* a major shareholder though.

During the ten-hour flight Juliana told him about her family — how 'fucked up' they all were. As a child she was miserable and lonely. "When Mummy died Daddy went to pieces. He really loved her. She was his third wife, and *totally* unsuitable." Michael noticed she had a way of exaggerating certain words when she spoke. "They met at a party in Chelsea. Mummy was a lot younger and came from an artistic family; my grandfather was friends with Lucian Freud. I posed for him you know. What an experience *that* was! The painting's in the Met… Or is it the Guggenheim? I can never remember which. Anyway, after Mummy died Daddy had no idea what to do with me so I was packed off to a succession of boarding schools." She sighed. "One miserable experience after another... I know what you're thinking; poor little rich girl, right? I admit it. I'm a cliché. As for my ancestors! Well, you know what a bunch decadents *they* were." She knocked back her third Bloody Mary. "What about your lot?"

Michael told her about Bartholomew; how, once freed from the Francome sugarcane estate he had made his way to Liverpool onboard a merchant ship; how he'd married an English girl and made the country his home. "It all started with him really; the Taylor dynasty. Well, you can hardly call it a dynasty."

"Yes, Daddy said we used to own him… Oh God. Sorry. That came out all wrong… That he was a slave on one of our plantations."

"No, no. You're right. You did own him."

She gave a cheeky mea culpa cringe, her huge eyes widening. "Terrible human beings aren't they." She sipped her drink, leaving a blood-red tinge around her lips. "So our families are connected then. Incredible isn't it. I mean, who would have thought that over century later you and I would be flying back to where it all began."

The flight touched down at Sangster Airport at 4.05 p.m. Michael had been to the Caribbean before — Barbados, St. Lucia, St, Kitts — but it was his first time in Jamaica.

When he stepped off the plane there was no feeling of 'coming home' like he'd often read about; he only ever felt that whenever he returned to Britain. What he did feel, though, was an odd sense of freedom.

They were met in the Arrival's Hall by a tall pot-bellied black man wearing shorts, t-shirt and a battered straw hat. He was around sixty years old and walked with a slight limp.

Juliana ran up and threw her arms around him "Clovis! Lovely to see you! How long has it *beeeen?*

"Three years, Miss."

"Three years! *Fuck!* How's Rose?"

"Oh she's fine. Lookin' forward ta seeing ya."

His rich Jamaican accent transported Michael back to his childhood, to the old Methodist church in Levenshulme where all the West Indians used to gather for Sunday worship: he would sit listening to the men chatting, fascinated by their strange accents, accents that were so different from his father's.

Juliana patted Clovis's pot belly. "What's *this?*"

He laughed. "Time catches up with us all ya know. 'Cept you. Ya've grown into a real beauty."

Juliana turned to Michael. "Don't you just love him!.. Clovis, this is—"

"Oh I know who this is, Miss." He removed his hat and took a step forward, offering his hand shyly. "Very pleased to meet ya, Prime Minista."

"This is Clovis, Michael. Our caretaker. He's been looking after the house since before I was born."

Michael shook his hand; the palm was rough and calloused.

"The pleasure's all mine, Clovis."

Clovis beamed. "Well now would ya look at dat.

Never did I tink I would be shakin' 'ands with a British Prime Minista! Not in my entire life."

Out of the corner of his eye Michael saw Reg and Gavin watching the encounter from the corner of the Arrivals Hall.

Oh piss off!

The moment they walked outside they were hit by a wall of tropical heat. The air was hot and sticky, the sunlight overwhelming.

Clovis led them to a silver minibus parked nearby. The pick-up point was full of people noisily piling into buses, cars and taxis.

"I hope it's got air-con," said Michael.

"It 'as sir, yes."

As Clovis slid open the side door, Juliana teased, "You wouldn't think his ancestors came from Jamaica would you Clovis?"

"Dat's right. I read *all* about it in the *Gleaner.* Welcome 'ome, sir."

A stickler for the facts, Michael wanted to say his ancestors were originally from the Gold Coast. Then again, going back even further, to Africa's Rift Valley; and before that, 450 million years ago, had crawled out of the sea along with everyone else. Instead he just smiled. "Thank you."

They left the airport, joined the A1 and headed east along the coast road. St. Ann's Bay was around 80 kilometers away. Before sitting back to enjoy the ride Michael glanced behind him and saw Reg and Gavin tailing them in a dark blue sedan. Which reminded him. He nudged Juliana. "Your father told me he used a private security firm when he was here. Where are they?"

"They'll be at the house when we get there." She patted his hand. "Chill out. You're on holiday." She glanced through the window at the dazzling Caribbean Sea. "Look at that view!" She leaned forward and put her head on Clovis's shoulder. "I've missed this place."

"No-weir lak it on Earth ya know."

When they reached St. Ann's Bay they took a right and drove south through the centre of town. At the end of Market Street they swung left onto Marcus Garvey Way.

Clovis pointed to a modest house on the right. "See dare, Prime Minista: 'de birthplace of our great statesman Marcus Garvey; 'im 'dat said 'Black skin is not a badge 'a shame, but rather a glorious symbol of national greatness'."

Michael looked at the house as they past. "I prefer 'If you have no confidence in self, you are twice defeated in the race of life'."

Clovis slapped the steering wheel in delight. "Amen to 'dat!"

"Never heard of him," said Juliana.

Michael chuckled, "And some fell on stony ground."

Clovis got the Biblical gag, smiling at Michael in the rearview mirror.

Marcus Garvey Way suddenly became Lime

Hall Road.

"Amazing," said Michael. "The first house I bought in Wilmslow was on Hall Road."

They continued on, breaking into open countryside.

Juliana motioned at the endless fields either side of the road. "All this land used to be the Francome sugarcane plantation. As you can see it's all overgrown now."

Michael pictured what it must have looked like back then; hundreds of slaves cutting sugarcane in the intense heat, loading it onto carts; the noise, the dust, the flies. He saw the overseer on his horse patrolling the fields, a coiled bullwhip attached to his saddle.

A kilometer further Clovis turned right and headed down a bumpy narrow track lined with tropical trees and bushes.

"Have they still not fixed this road yet!?" asked Juliana indignantly, her light frame thrown around in the back.

"No, Miss. Coun-sil don't give a damn. Wa need someone lak you, Prime Minista, 'ta shake 'tings up."

"I'll put my name forward," joked Michael

Juliana laughed, "They couldn't afford you."

"Listen to the heiress! How much is your family worth? A billion?"

She grinned "Two point four, actually!"

The road widened as they drove towards a set of gates. Behind them was a large plantation house partially screened by Blue Mahoe trees. Painted white, it was made of wood and had a cedar shingled roof. A veranda ran along the whole length of the ground floor. Softening either side of the house were huge bougainvillea bushes bursting with yellow flowers.

Clovis opened the door of the minibus but Michael beat him to it; he jumped out, walked over and opened the gates.

Clovis turned to Juliana. "Well, would ya look at 'dat now! Wait till 'a tell Rose."

As Michael waved them through, Reg and Gavin pulled up in their rented sedan. Winding down the window Reg took in the house and grounds. "Security nightmare, Prime Minister."

"Relax. No one knows I'm here."

Reg fixed him with a serious stare. "*Please!*"

Michael tried to make light of his naivety. "Then it's a good job you and are Gavin are here then, isn't it. I feel safer already… By the way, you're staying in one of the cottages on the estate. Clovis will sort you out after he's dropped us off… Hold on, who's this?"

A black Transit van raced up behind them. Gavin hurriedly opened the glove compartment and grabbed a Glock pistol, resting it in his lap.

The van came to a halt, kicking up a cloud of dust. Michael noticed the logo on the side — a pair of hands cupping the Island of Jamaica. A muscular, shaven-headed black man wearing combat pants and a black t-shirt got out, a holstered pistol strapped to his hip

"Sorry we're late, sir. I'm Justin: Island Security"

"Great to meet you, Justin. Glad you made it" He motioned to the sedan. "Reg and Gavin: my security team from the UK. Liaise with them would you."

"Yes, sir."

Michael smiled at Reg. "Happy now?"

He walked back to the minibus and got in.

Clovis drove another hundred meters, skirting a circular patch of lawn with a sun dial at its centre before the minibus came to halt in front of the house.

Juliana sighed. "Finally!"

"Gorgeous place," said Michael. He noticed half a dozen humming birds hovering around the bougainvillea. "So peaceful. Is this where the plantation manager used to live?"

"Dat's right, sir."

"Please call me Michael.

"Right ya are."

Juliana slid open the minibus door and jumped out. A plump, diminutive black lady in her sixties wearing a bright orange dress came rushing out of the house. She hurried across the veranda, ran up to Juliana and gave her a hug.

"You are a sight for sore eyes! Welcome back! 'Bin too long. Too long!"

"You know how it is. How are you Rose?"

"Fine, darlin', fine… Cum in. Ya must be tired so ya must."

Juliana and Grace disappeared into the house.

Clovis looked at Michael and smiled. "'Tick as 'tieves those two… 'Diss way."

They walked up a set of wooden steps, crossed the verandah and entered the cool, spacious hall. Sunlight filtered in through closed shutters. A ceiling fan above them whirled. The mahogany floor was highly polished and held the patina of generations. Dotted around the room were Jacobean side tables with barley twist legs, Georgian oil lamps and blue and white Chinese vases atop their dark surfaces. Above, oil paintings in gold frames were hung on the oak-panelled walls. A grandfather clock ticked lazily in the shadows. The house hadn't change in over two hundred years.

Michael shook his head. "What an incredible atmosphere."

"'Sumtimes, when I'm 'ear on my own, I 'ave a feelin' I'm walkin' among ghosts."

Michael shivered.

A voice came from the next room. "Clovis! What ya doin' mon!?"

Clovis raised his eyes and whispered. "Women! 'Ave us on a string they do. I 'ear dat!"

Michael gave a mock grimace, and like two naughty boys they made their way into the Edwardian sitting room that opened onto the rear of the house where Juliana and Rose were relaxing on rattan easy chairs sipping lemonade

Walking out onto the veranda Michael went to the edge of the rail and looked down. A gentle breeze ruffled his open-neck white shirt. From the elevated position it was as if the house was floating on a sea of tropical greenery. “Marvellous view!”

“Stop acting like a tourist and have some of Rose’s *gorgeous* lemonade,” chided Juliana.

Rose lifted the glass pitcher. As she was filling Michael’s glass Clovis said, “I’ll take ‘da two gentlemen to de overseer’s cottage.”

Michael sat down. “Very apt… Thank you, Clovis.”

“What are ‘dare names, Michael?”

Rose was apoplectic. “‘Michael’! ‘Michael!’ Have ya no respect! It’s Prime Minista’!”

“’Im already told me ta call ‘im dat!”

Michael rushed to his defence. “It’s OK Rose… It’s Reg and Gavin, Clovis.”

“Reg and Gavin. Right ya-ar.” Before leaving he gave Rose a withering look. ”See! Interfering old busybod—“

“’Nuff of dat now! On ya way.”

Rose handed Michael his glass of homemade lemonade and smiled. “Joys ‘a married life. Can’t beat it.” She put the pitcher down on the rattan table. “I’ll leave ya ‘t-enjoy yar ‘oliday. Shout me if ya need anytin’.”

Juliana sat back in her chair. “Thanks Rose.”

Dogs were barking. Michael snapped awake. It was night, the bedroom pitch black. An eerie orange glow danced across the wall. He jumped out of bed and went to the window. Beneath a cloudy sky he could see the whole of the plantation. A group of men brandishing flaming torches were walking across the sugarcane fields. They were heading towards a dark forest of palm trees with a pack of howling dogs. Suddenly the moon appeared from behind a cloud. One of the men looked back at the house and saw him standing at the window.

"A slave's escaped, sir!" he shouted. "The trouble-causer; Bartholomew!"

Another of the men yelled, "There he is!" and let the dogs off the leash. The dogs ran into the undergrowth. Moments later there was a spine-chilling scream.

BANG! BANG! BANG! A voice called out, "What's wrong?"

Michael woke up just as his bedroom door swung open. Juliana rushed in wearing a t-shirt, her bare legs glowing in the dawn light.

"Are you alright? You woke me up. I thought you were being attacked."

He sat up, his body drenched in sweat. "I was having a nightmare." He pointed at the window. "I was standing right there, watching some men chasing a slave across the plantation. It was horrible."

"It's your own fault. That's all you talked about last night."

His mind went back to the previous evening; after dinner he and Juliana sat on the veranda with Clovis and Rose.

"You were asking Clovis about the history of the estate. *Fuck* knows why. Depressing subject. But no, *you* wanted to know every last detail; where the slaves were kept; what they ate; what happened when they tried to escape. And when he told you you were staying in the plantation manager's bedroom you were ecstatic. So serves you right."

Michael sighed. He could still hear the screams. "But that's the reason I came here; to find out about my ancestor."

"Not all in one night! No wonder you had nightmares."

"Oh God. Bore everyone did I?"

"Senseless!"

Juliana sat on the edge of the bed; a curtainless four-poster. Her tone softened and a sparkle came into her eyes. "Anyway, I don't know about you, but *I* came here to have fun."

"Here you are."

Michael had to shield his eyes from the intense sunlight. Juliana was standing in front of him wearing a tiny pink bikini. She was holding two rum cocktails. Behind her the Caribbean washed gently ashore.

"Thanks." Raising himself up off the sun lounger he took a drink and looked out to sea. "Wow, it's hot."

She sat on the lounger next to him. "Just a bit." She put the straw in her mouth and took a long sip. *"Ummmm*! Delish."

After breakfast they had driven along the coast

to a secluded cove belonging to a 5-star hotel. The beach was almost deserted, apart from a few white couples sunbathing. A small cocktail bar shaded by palm trees nestled against the base of the cliff. Although Reg and Gavin were nowhere to be seen, Michael could sense they were around, spying on him from the shadows.

They weren't the only ones.

"You're not in bad shape are you," said Juliana, eyeing his bare torso.

"Thanks."

"For an old guy."

"Cheeky." He returned the favour, scanning her delicate frame, from the tip of her tufted blonde hair to her painted toes. He noticed she had a powder-blue seahorse tattooed on her left ankle. *Very sexy.* "You need a good meal inside you."

Juliana lay back on the sun lounger, tipping her Dior glasses over her eyes. "Perfection, darling. Sheer perfection."

A lone frigate bird swooped low over the water. Michael watched as it angled its body before flying out to sea. Westminster was a million miles away. He closed his eyes.

"Michael?"

"Um?

Juliana was lying on her stomach. She handed him a bottle of sunscreen. "Would you mind?"

"Sure."

He sat up. Juliana reached behind and undid

the knot of her bikini top. He squeezed the bottle, dribbling the lotion in a long line all the way down her back. Taking his time, he began massaging her neck and shoulders, expertly pressing his palms and thumbs into her snowy-white flesh.

"You've done this before," said Juliana.

"Once or twice."

His hands slid down her body, massaging every inch as they descended. The vertebra of her spine were like stepping stones. He caressed the outline of her ribs,

"*Umm.* Heaven."

"You've got beautiful skin." he said, his voice thickening.

"Thank you."

His hands narrowed as they hugged the contours of her waist, curving outwards over her hips, rising to her delicious, almost-naked bottom. He felt himself getting hard. She seemed to guess what he was thinking.

"Do my bum would you."

They fell into the room, crashing onto the bed. Coiled around each other he was eating her alive. She slid her tongue from his mouth and pressed it to his ear. "Fuck me." He knelt up, breathless, his eyes blazing. She glared at him. "Do anything you want to me." He scrambled off his t-shirt and rolled her onto her back. Reaching down he undid both strings of her bikini, her naked body revealed like a long-awaited gift. She was right; sheer perfection. He drank in every inch of her flesh. *Fuuuuck!* He got off the bed, took off his shorts and stood there.

"Suck my cock."

Her inert body suddenly came to life. She turned over and sat up. She took in its full throbbing length. She grinned and made herself comfortable, snuggling her bottom into the sheets. Taking hold of his cock she wanked it slowly, rhythmically, her huge eyes locked onto his. She opened her mouth and was about to slide it in when she stopped.

The wait was agonizing. "Suck it… Please."

She looked at him, a mischievous expression on her face. "Let's play a game. Let's pretend its fuck knows how many years ago. I'm Lady Francome, yeah, visiting my Jamaican estate, and you're one of the grooms. I've seen you in the stables, brushing down one of the horse, your muscular black body covered in sweat. You look at me and I melt. I'm desperate to fuck you. I pass you a note, begging you to come to my bedroom at midnight. So I'm lying here, waiting. My pussy's soaking wet. The clock chimes midnight. Suddenly there's a knock on the door. I say 'Come in,' softly like that…"

Michael was hypnotised. He swallowed hard. "And?"

"…The door opens and there you are, a hungry look on your face, your gorgeous black muscles rippling in the candlelight. I say, 'Yes?' all innocent. And you say—"

"Take off your chemise."

Juliana was delighted he was playing along. "So I do as I'm told… You stare at my gorgeous white body. You've never seen anything so beautiful in your whole life. You'd be killed if you were found in here, but that only adds to the excitement. Suddenly your cock goes hard, just like it is now." She took hold of his cock and carried on wanking. "Umm. Nice... " Finally she slipped the whole length into her mouth.

He shivered. "Oh Ju-Ju… Oh… Suck it… That's right… Oh you're so fucking sexy."

She spat on his cock, "Ha!" sucking even harder.

He pushed the fragile heiress onto her back. A circle was closing. He knelt beside the bed and slid his face between her thighs, licking his way towards her blonde pussy. He paused to inhale its fragrance. He prised his tongue deep inside, making her shiver. She groaned as he circled her moist, inner walls, cresting her salty pearls.

"Oh... Oh Michael."

The fact the she was younger than his daughter never registered. Lust had him by the throat. He got up, climbed onto the bed and leaned over her menacingly, his head inches from hers. He stared into her baby-blue eyes.

"You want me, don't you?"

"I *fucking* want you!"

He wrapped her legs around his waist and slipped his cock inside her.

"Ohhhh…."

Her pussy was like liquid velvet. He began with gentle thrusts, increasing the speed as her eyes widened. He stopped, braced himself, then hammered into her, nailing the forbidden fruit to the bed. She opened her mouth in ecstasy.

"Oh God oh God oh God oh God oh God…"

XXVI

TRENCHTOWN REGGAE thundered through a boombox as cars and trucks roared along the highway. It was shortly after midday. They were sitting at a roadside Jerk shack sipping ice-cold beer. Juliana had her feet on the tin chair next to him. She wore a purple sarong over a pink bikini, her orange flip flops moving to the beat. At Reg's insistence Michael wore a baseball cap and black shades. And it seemed to work. So far, after two weeks on the island, he hadn't been recognised once.

They were on their way to Montego Bay when Juliana suggested stopping at one of her father's favourite haunts — 'Celine's'. "You simply *have* to try it." Famous for serving the spiciest Jerk chicken on the island, the eponymous street food eatery was owned and run by formidable Jamaican lady in her fifties.

Michael had to shout above the din. "Your father was right. I like spicy food, but *that* was ridiculous! My mouth's still on fire."

Juliana leaned across and kissed him lovingly on the cheek. "Poor thing."

He squeezed her hand, whispering, "Darling Ju-Ju."

The past fortnight was full of such affectionate little gestures.

From the moment they slept together they were

inseparable. Every day, after breakfast, Juliana drove him to one of her favourite places — secluded coves, local bars, artisan markets, restaurants, trendy boutiques. To the locals they were just another honeymoon couple, holding hands in the street, smooching on café terraces. Michael knew Reg and Gavin were watching, but he didn't care. He was free; free from all responsibility; free from being… well… Michael Taylor. Returning to the house they took romantic walks around the grounds, the evening air filled with the intoxicating scent of tropical flowers. After several rum cocktails on the veranda they headed for the bedroom to make love.

Juliana motioned to her open-top jeep parked nearby. "Shall we?"

Michael nodded.

Half an hour later they pulled into Montego Bay. She drove down to the harbor where her father kept a power boat. *Juliana* was tied up half way along the jetty, a sleek, twin-engine craft beloved of drug-runners intent on outpacing the coastguard.

Michael stared at the powerful machine. "Sure you can handle it?"

Juliana smiled. "Just get onboard." She walked to the back of the boat, got behind the wheel and slid the key into the ignition. "I'll show you if I can handle it."

She started the engines, easing her namesake towards the mouth of the harbor. Michael looked back to see Reg and Gavin standing forlornly on the jetty. Reg gave a 'What the fuck!' gesture. Michael signaled him to calm down.

Once past the harbor's outer walls Juliana opened the throttle. There was a roar as both engines kicked in. The boat reared up, throwing Michael against the side.

"Fuck!"

"Sorry!" shouted Juliana, smirking. "I should have warned you!"

They headed out to sea in a buffeting of wind, spray and sunlight.

"Enjoying it?"

Michael turned to look at his skipper. "Loving it!"

Gradually Montego Bay faded into the distance. Apart from a cargo ship on the horizon they were alone in vastness of the Caribbean. Eventually Juliana throttled back and they came to a halt, leaving them bobbing in the water.

She came from behind the wheel and pressed herself against him. "Make love to me."

Later that night unanswered questions hovered over the dinner table; questions about the future. There were dining at Sugar Mill, an award-winning restaurant located on the Half Moon Golf Course. With its immaculate white linen tablecloths and subdued lighting it was the polar opposite of Celine's Jerk Shack. As was the menu. Michael had Lobster Thermidor; Juliana Blackened Fillet of Sea

Bass. Although it tasted delicious their minds were elsewhere.

Juliana was the first to broach the subject. She picked up her wine glass, stared at the tablecloth and asked, hesitantly. "Is this a holiday romance then?"

The answer she got caused her to raise her head.

"Oh no, Juliana. Far from it."

Her pretty face beamed. "I'm *so* glad you said that." She reached across the table and took his hand. "Michael, I love you."

"Hey. Let's not get ahead of ourselves."

"What does *that* mean? Don't you like me?

"Of *course* I like you. You're absolutely gorgeous!" He squeezed her hand. "Let's see what happens when we get back to the UK."

Her eyes lit up. "Really! We'll carry on seeing each other? Do you *mean* it?"

"Every word."

She was ecstatic. "Oh my *God* I'm *so* happy!" Reality gate-crashed. "Hold on. What about your wife?"

"Let me deal with Sadie."

A grim-face Reg approached the table.

"You need to come with me, Prime Minister."

Michael glanced at Juliana. "Sorry about this."

He got up and followed Reg outside. "What's going on?"

"You're wanted back to the UK. MI5 have credible evidence there's about to be a military coup."

"A what!?"

"A military coup, sir."

Michael couldn't believe what he was hearing. "You *are* joking? What are we, some banana repub—"

"You have to take this seriously, Prime Minister! Nothing's happened yet, but you need to return to stabilise the situation. MI5 think there's a greater risk if you remain outside the country. You're booked on the first flight out tomorrow morning."

Michael shook his head and sighed. "I've no choice then?"

"Not really."

"Shit!.. Very well, I'll settle the bill and fetch Lady Francome."

Dawn light filtered through the shutters. Michael stared at Juliana lying next to him; she was fast asleep without a care in the world. He thought about Sadie, about how she'd react when he told her he wanted a divorce. *She'll probably be relieved.* Things hadn't been right for a while. He was convinced she was having an affair. Recently she'd been spending a lot of time in Paris. *She's probably seeing her ex.* He wondered why, when two people got married, things always turned out this way. He thought about his mum and dad staying together all those years. Till Death Do Us Part. It was all so different back then. The past haunted him, however much he tried to deny it.

He carefully pulled back the sheet so as not to disturb her, but Juliana woke up. Realising he was about to leave she flung her arms around him and held him tightly.

"Don't go."

"I *have* to."

"Let me driving you to the airport then."

He kissed her on the cheek. "No. You stay here."

"That's not an offer Michael. I'm driving you."

Michael smiled. "OK."

They got up and began to get dressed.

After breakfast Michael said his goodbyes to Rose and Clovis. "Thanks for looking after me. I've really enjoyed my stay."

Rose gave him a withering look. "You English! Ya so cold." She opened her arms. "Cum 'ere. Gimmie a proper hug."

Michael put his arms around her and squeezed her tight.

"Dat's better! Cum back soon now!"

"Thanks. I will."

Reg and Gavin were on the veranda when they walked outside. They watched Michael put his suitcase in the back of Juliana's Jeep.

"See you at the airport, Prime Minister," said Reg, walking to the sedan.

"See you there."

Juliana opened the door and put the roof down. "All set?"

He nodded. They climbed into the Jeep. Juliana put the key in the ignition.

"Let's get married."

"Whoa! Don't you think we shouldn't live together first?"

For a brief moment he imagined what that would mean; he'd be a member of the Francome family, and by virtue the master of this house… the plantation manager's house. How often must his ancestors have looked at this place with a mixture of fear and envy as they toiled in the fields? And what would Bartholomew make of it?

Suddenly a voice came into his head.

"Do it, Mi-kel. We deserve it."

Time really is the washing machine of history.

"We love each other, Michael. So why wait."

Her youthful exuberance amused him.

"You *do* know I've been married twice."

"So what?" She grinned. "You know what they say: third time luck—"

"This is the BBC News. Early this morning the Prime Minister was killed in a car bomb. He was staying at the holiday home of Lord Francome in Jamaica when the car he was traveling in exploded. Also killed was Lord Francome's nineteen-year-old daughter, Lady Juliana Francome. The Prime Minister's bodyguards were severely injured. Both men were taken to hospital in Montego Bay and are said to be in a critical condition. So far no one has claimed responsibility. Tributes have been pouring in from world leaders. The United States President, Kirsty MacLean, described Michael Taylor as a visionary and a patriot. Italy's President Angelo Scarpi said that Europe had lost its torch-bearer. Meanwhile, the

Home Secretary and Deputy Prime Minister Grace Magars has taken over as leader and declared a state of emergency. In her first address to the nation from Downing Street this morning she called for calm.

XXVII

One Year Later

"HURRY UP for fuck's sake! The bastards are getting away!" Haley picked up a crowbar, prised open the crate of RPGs and handed one to Jim. He fixed it to the end of the rocket launcher, aimed and fired. Seconds later there was an almightily explosion.

"*Whoa!!!*"

"When the smoke cleared Haley peered through her binoculars. The truck had been completely destroyed, mangled body parts strewn across the road. She saw a man crawl from the wreckage; hauling himself to his feet he was stumbling towards the burnt-out shell of Kings Walk Shopping Mall.

"I'm on it!" Haley grabbed her pistol, jumped over the wall and ran towards him.

Exhausted, the man fell to the ground, rolling onto his back. She slowed her pace and released the safety catch. She glanced up and down the Kings Road checking none of his fellow fascists were around. The whole of Chelsea was a battle-scarred landscape. She pictured what it was like before the civil war; she and Lonny often came here on a Saturday to cement their hatred of the rich. Poor Lonny, killed two weeks ago in a botched attempt to storm Euston Station, another fascist stronghold.

She stood over the man lying on the ground. He was Asian, around twenty-years old. His handsome face was blooded, his bulging eyes staring up at her in absolute terror. For a moment she thought it was her ex-boyfriend Saleem. But no, it wasn't. Then she noticed the insignia on the breast pocket of his combat fatigues — a golden acorn surrounded by a cluster of oak leaves.

She cocked her pistol, pointed it at the man's head and spat, "GB *fucking* Patriots! You're a patriot, are you? Well a lot of good it's done you.

"Please," he panted. "Please don't—"

She pulled the trigger and watched his head explode. "Fascist cunt."

Jim shouted from behind the wall. "Haley! We need to get out of here!"

She walked back across the Kings Road. She thought about her father; his death had been the catalyst of all this destruction. As to who carried out the assassination, well, that was a mystery. The suspect list was long and varied — M15, disgruntled cabinet colleagues, the socialist leader of the military coup Colonel Tim Havers, a mysterious Marxist collective with ties to the Kremlin, ISIS. There was even a rumor that an Albanian people-smuggling king pin had ordered his death so that the lucrative trade could start again.

After a year of civil war in which the country had torn itself apart there was stalemate. More entrenched than ever, each side was convinced right was on their side. But the day was drawing near when a huge battle would take place to decide the fate of the United Kingdom.

Approaching her fellow fighters on the other side of the wall, Haley glanced back at the man lying dead in the street. From out of nowhere the chorus of Lonny's favourite anti-fascist song by Billy Bragg came into her head, and she began to sing it at the top of her voice.

Other Novels by Malcolm Storer

The Cure

Inside The Cheshire Set

The Tenants

Printed in Great Britain
by Amazon

60240502R10170